How I Became the God of Honor

God of Honor

To Kyle

Please Enjoy The Read
and Let Me know what you
Think

[signature]

By D. E. Richardson

Prefect

I was born third to a family of farmers. I was named Bill after an uncle who died some years earlier. My father believed in one principle above all else and that was Honor! Well, that's not quite right, he believes in God which just reinforces honor. I found an old sword (plastic) when I was three and just fell in love with weapons, not guns and tanks but hand weapons like knives, pikes, staffs, ect, you get the idea. My father also believed that there is no such thing as the best; it was ok to be beaten by someone better, which just showed you, that you had work to do. I didn't think about it growing up that the world didn't follow the same rules as our family, but I would get up in the morning and get ready for school, dad was normally gone by then. After school there were chores, home work and then practice with the weapon of the day. As I got better then my teachers, Father would find a better one to take his or her place. By the time I was sixteen I was band from most competitions because of my skill level. By age twenty I was known to be one of a handful that was considered the best in hand wielded weapons.

I would travel the world to show and sell some of the best hand wielded weapons in the world, but I still did not own one myself. I was twenty-one when I got the call of dad being sick, he had been sick a long time but I wasn't told, He had made a turn for the worst, so the call went out come home now. I had been sending money home since I was eighteen to help out. There was still four at home, eight all to gather plus grandkids; I figured they needed all the help they could get. I was in Main so I caught the first flight back to Dodge City, Kansas. Where one of my brothers picked me up and we drove back to Moscow, Kansas about 60 miles away. Moscow is a little town that is in the middle of nowhere, and yet it is the only place I call home. We went to visit Father the next day, Moscow doesn't have a hospital so we went back to Dodge City, he talked to us while we were there, joked and reminisced, I could tell when he got tired but wouldn't let the nurse chase us out. But after awhile mom did the chasing, but as I was leaving dad called me back in, mom and him had a silent talk with their eyes for a minute or two, I guess father won because mom said, "not too long you two," as she let herself out. I went back to his bed and pulled up a chair.

He said, "I am very proud of the man you have become, I haven't said that enough to you but I thought you should know before it is too late."

Tears started coming to my eye's he was looking at the ceiling when I looked over to him, I could tell this was hard on him as well so I didn't interrupt him as he went on, "your birthday is in three mouth from yesterday, I know this is a lot of trouble for you but I don't think that your mom should do it, I have a gift for you coming to the house the week of your birthday I don't know what day but if you could be there I would really appreciate it?" He then looked at me like he was afraid I would turn him down, I would move the world if he ask for it, so I laugh a little then said, "Is that all I would be honored to be there and besides it for me isn't it."

He relaxed then and said, "good now go get your mother you know she is a nervous wreck in the hall right now.

I said, "Why didn't she stay here?"

He said; "she said this is father son business so she left." He shrugged "you know your mom!" I laughed as I got up and left the room. He died two days later. I cancelled everything and stayed with mom after the funeral, the day of my birthday it came, a wood crate just two foot by two foot by five foot, I had to prove who I was, and that father had died, sign a load of papers, before the guy would give me the box, and I still didn't think he was going to give it to me when he made a phone call to someone and I heard the guy on the other end say it is going to the guy in front of you it is his now give him the box and get back here you have other deliveries to make. He gave me the box took all the paper work and left. I walked into the living room with it in my arm when mom seen it she said, "Not in here go to the garage to open that," pointing out the door. She would not let anyone go with me she said; "this is time for you and your father." I didn't understand and no one else did ether but mom has spoken and now it is law! I took it to the garage which was good I needed a crowbar to open it up when I did I couldn't believe my eyes, it was a Japanese sword with sheath, no paper work or letter but still one of the best swords I have ever seen and as I said before I have seen the best in the world. I thought of father and began to cry.

Father and mother didn't spend the money I was sending home, they saved it all tell they had enough to buy the sword. It took me a month to get that much out of my mother but no more when that info came out she told me that was enough and the subject was closed. So where it came from; what it is, its name, all are mysteries to me still. I finally went back to work and my apartment that I hadn't seen in almost a year. Things got back to normal, I spent time with my new sword till it became a part of my arm it felt right there as I moved it in the practice arcs and exercises.

Then came the day that the gun and knife show came to my town, I took this as a opportunity to see if I could find out more on my sword so I strapped it on and went to the show. I saw him before he saw me, he looked out of place standing in one corner looking at every one he could see, he made me uncomfortable so I was just turning down a different row when he saw me, and he did a double take then headed my way. I didn't know what to do, plus I was kind of curious what he wanted myself. The closer he got the more he stared, but when he got in front of me he said with a grin on his face; "it is you my lord I had lost faith that you would come, but here you are." He began to walk around me as he talked; "my lord you are just as they said you would be and there is the famous sword that was your companion in yours travels. I never thought I would be the one you would show yourself to, but here you are." He got a little closer then I liked and I put out a hand to stop his progress. He looked at it a minute with a puzzling look then the smile came back and he started bobbing his head up and down saying, "yes your right I am sorry I am here to deliver this back to you aren't I, my lord I ask you to forgive an old man his babbling." From somewhere in his shirt he produced a round piece of gold with a ribbon connected to it he hung the ribbon on my arm. I pulled my arm back and began to look at the medal when I realized that it was real gold not a fake I looked up to find the man walking off I yelled; "hey mister what is this?"

The man stopped in mid step. He turned around with what looked like fear on his face, he ran back to me and bowed, yes I said bowed!

He said, "My lord I am sorry I meant no harm please don't hold my lapse in my duty to my family, I was just excited to see you and to know the stories of my family are real."

I said, "Look I don't know what this is all about but this is real…."

He cut me off when he said, "Yes my lord to activate it you just need to say, by my honor I will protect and teach honor where ever and whenever it is needed."

People where beginning to gather around us and talk, I looked around at the faces but all I could say was; "by my honor…" he cut me off again "not here my lord when you are alone," then it was like a slap in his face when he stopped bowed again saying, "I am sorry my lord please forgive my outburst I don't mean to tell my lord what to do but I was just surprised you would start it here please be sure to have your sword at your side when you repeat this chant. As always my family and I will always be yours to command, but at this time I must go as was told for so long may your travels be safe my lord" with that he bowed turned and ran from the building, all I could do was shrug at the crowd who laughed then began to break up. I had enough myself and I headed home.

When I got home I showered and shaved, comb my hair and put on a new pair of pants, fixed a quick snack to eat, when I set down to tie my boots I realized I had just dressed for the mountains, hiking boots and all. I looked at the medal setting on the table and said; "I guess I am going to try you out what's the worst I look foolish I don't have to tell anyone." I strapped the sword on my waist, pack the place up like I was going on a trip then at the last minute call Jane my secretary told her, "I think I am going to have to make a trip don't know for how long?"

She asked, "Is it your mom?"

I said, "No but please cover for me and I will call you when I get back first thing."

She said, "She would take care of things here and be safe." We said, "Goodbye" and I hung up the phone. I don't know why but I then called my mom and told her "I would be out of touch for awhile so don't worry." When I hung up that time I felt I had done what I needed to before, before what? What was I expecting here some old man gives a medal and implies it is magic and I get excited! Well it is gold nobody gives that away for a prank, and I just realized I was excited. I stood in the middle of the room, patted myself down to be sure I didn't forget something, check the buckle on the sword, adjusted the medal around my neck, stood straight and said to the wall;

WITH MY HONOR I WILL PROTECT AND TEACH HONOR WHERE EVER AND WHENEVER IT IS NEEDED!

Chapter 1

"That was a disappointing," I said to the wall, "nothing happened," but that wasn't my wall, I turned to see I was in an ally- way between two building. When did that happened? Did I close my eyes for a second, I didn't think so. I looked up to the sky it was high about noon here I think, I could hear only one sound, someone yelling, I couldn't understand the language, maybe I was too far away, I began to walk to the end of the ally, when I was close enough I looked around the corner. The street was dirt I was just off of the main square where two groups of people had congregated; one looked like the residents and the other military. The residents were scared with the military scattered around them in a circle. The noise was coming from a commander I took it yelling and kicking an old man that was in the dirt at his feet. I was just going to watch it not like I can take on an army even one with only twenty or so guys in it. Then the commander took his sword out he was planning to kill this old man, "there is no honor in that" I said as I walked out straight for the crowd. I passed the first solder before anyone seen me coming, he jumped back pulling his sword but I had already moved on. I got to the old man just as the commander brought his arm down for the killing blow, was he surprised when steel hit steel, he followed his sword down then mine back to me smiling at him, I said, "now there is no honor killing a man with no weapon!"

He back up and said something I am sure was not nice then squared with me and the fight was on. He wasn't very good, my brother could have bet him, his skill level was just better then beginner, I let him chop for a little so I could be sure he didn't have more skill then he was showing, he didn't I finally got board so I waited for a chance, when it came I flipped his sword around breaking his hold on the handle then flipped it away, it flew higher than I expected the crowed split to get out of the way of the falling sword, he watched it sail till it hit the ground when he turned his head back to me he found my sword tip at his neck, I said, "give up or die!" I already knew he didn't understand but he got the point and knelt on the ground. He started to put his head on down I put the tip of my sword under his chin and made him point his head up to where he could see me as I shook my head no, resting my sword there on his shoulder I looked around, all eyes were on me, some with hope some with fear, now what I said, to myself "you are in the middle of a fight, don't speak the language, don't even know what side is right here." I seen his sword in the dirt again, I said "that is no way to treat a fine sword" I put my sword down walked over to his sword picked it up and turned it back and forth studying the workmanship of the blade, I walked back over in front of him I told him "that it was a fine blade," he still didn't understand I said, "give me the sheath"! I took my sword and tapped the sheath buckled to his waist, he finally got the idea and unbuckled the belt and handed it to me, I took it buckled it to my belt took a rag I carry for my sword and wiped the blade down one side then up the other before putting the sword in the sheath, I turned back to him I said; "now what to do with you?" I looked around again that is when I noticed two things I didn't notice before one was a well, that is when my mouth went dry; the second was a group of young women dress differently than the rest of the crowd. There was only twelve of them aged between I guessed thirty and six separated from everyone else, I pointed to this group then made a gesture for one to come to me. One of them looked around then came meekly over to me, she was probably my age or close anyway, I pointed to the well then made a drinking movement. She looked surprised for a moment then shook her head yes, she ran off but not to the well but to one of the houses when she came back she had a small cup, she handed me the cup and bowed at the same time, I took the cup thank her and bowed just a little back at her, the cup being small I thought maybe the well was dry and I am drinking their water supply I drank the cup full before tasting it that was a mistake, when the burning started it took my breath away, I started coughing I dropped the cup and it broke my eyes started watering, I thought I had just been poisoned, the commander started to move I put my sword back on his shoulder, he stopped some of the crowd laughed, I looked back at the girl who was scared she didn't know whether to run or just die on the spot, I pointed again to the well this time I took her chin in my hand and turned it to see what I was pointing at. She started yelling something two more girls ran to the well pulled up a bucket then brought a cup that they pulled from the bucket. When they got there they gave it to the girl who then offered it to me with head bowed this time I didn't bow back, I took a small taste before drinking it all, yes it was water and good water at that. I gave the cup back to them, they ran to get me another cup, while they were filling the cup I thought this language thing is going to be a problem so what can I do to solve it, I remember a science study I was reading that said it is believed that our blood contains all of our traits and if we could unlock the code we could learn just by **sharing a drop or two of blood, it sounded like it** was worth a try and I like this girl who was brave enough to come to me when other won't. So when they got back with the cup I took the tip of my sword and pricked my finger, I then held it over the cup pinching my finger till five drops of blood dripped into the cup, mixing it with my sword tip I picked up the cup and in both hands I held it out to the girl and said out load (because I knew no one could understand what I was saying) a pray saying, "please lord let this work," the girl took it, the old man who had not made a sound sense this had started said something, I looked down at him to see him looking at the girl with wide eye's, when I looked back she was just taking the cup down, I looked at her a moment nothing, great just one more thing I failed at. That's when the commander tried to slide away again I thought I don't have time to keep chasing him down all over. So I turned to look at him moving my sword to cut a small red line in his neck also saying very calmly "If you move again I am going to cut your ears off put them in your pocket and string a rope through your ear hole and stake you down to the dirt." But while I was talking next to me I heard a small cry then talking at my feet the man got really scared and was lying on the ground covering his ears. I looked back to the voice at my feet it was the girl with her eyes shut, talking to the ground, I heard noise coming from the crowed when I looked around every one was on the ground like the girl this went for the solders too. I bent down touched the girl on the chin till she looked up.

I said, "You can understand me now can't you?" She nodded and the head went down to the ground again and I couldn't get it to come up, so I said, "you have been chosen may girl to be my

voice to all the people here so do you think my
voice they hear should come from the ground?"
She stayed like she was for a long time before she
lifted her head, I said, "Great so let's try standing
then." She shook her head but did get on her
knees. I said. "That will have to do for now. I
need to do the same thing with you so I can
understand when you talk so if you would get me
a cup of water we will try this again." I had to
smile when she got up and ran to the well pulled
up the bucket and filled the cup again, I didn't
think we had used a whole bucket of water for
two cups but that wasn't what I thought was
funny, the whole crowd watched her run over and
run back, she handed me the cup and knelt back
down, I said, "ok, I need your hand." I thought
there for a minute she wasn't going to give it to
me she kept looking at her hand then finally gave
it to me. I knelt down in front of her so we could
see eye to eye, she tried to lie down, I stopped her
by saying "don't lie down because I would look
foolish laying in front of you on the ground. Look
I am going to poke your finger like I did mine," I
held out my finger so she could see, "this will hurt
just a bit but not long and no harm or damage to

you or your finger, so are you ready then?" She shook her head yes so I took my sword tip again to prick her finger pinched it until a couple of drops of blood splashed in the cup, I wiped her finger with my fingers to be sure it had stop bleeding before letting her hand go, she looked at her finger then smiled when it didn't bleed even when she pinched it herself, I swished the cup around then drank the water, I didn't taste anything but water which was good I think it would have made a bad impression if I gagged when I drank it.

I said, "Ok, let me explain a few things; there are rules here and here they are. First only you can understand me, I have chosen you without you having a choice, for that I am sorry but that cannot be undone, but I cannot understand anyone else so you are my voice and ears. When I talk you will recite what I say word for word and when someone else is talking you will repeat it word for word to me, even if they call you a name you don't like, tell you not too, or threaten your family you will tell me all of it if you are translating for me, do you understand?" She shook her head yes. "If you cannot do this I need to know now, because if you cannot I picked the wrong woman for the job." A good sign I think because she didn't bow her head or try to lie down again instead she just kept looking at me when she said, "yes I can do it for you master."

"Great," I said without showing the surprise I felt because I understood her voice, "now rule two you need to pick at least one or two to help you in this I will make it so I can understand them but only you will understand me. But this rule is for all of you if I find out that anyone does not tell me something told to them for me or they tell something like I said it and I didn't. I will end this and the only way I know is death. This is not for status this is to help everyone here. So pick your helper's well."

She said in a low voice, "anyone?"

I said, "yes I will decide for myself if I accept them or not."

She nodded, "ok then let's get to work now stand up!"

This time she stood all the way up with me, I turned to her and said, "I need you to tell the group what I am about to say." She said she was ready. So, I said, "I have chosen this women," I turned to her and said in a lower voice "what is your name" she said her name but I knew I couldn't say the name but it sounded like Anna, so I stood up and said to the group again, "I have chosen Anna to be my voice and my ears, when she talks she will be saying what I am saying what she hears I will hear." There was a long gap after I quit talking before she started, she repeated every word but paused again at Anna but said it anyway, I realized my mistake after I heard her say it so I stopped her again this time I started by saying "I am sorry about your name you can still use it, I only said Anna because that is as close to your name as I heard so please forgive me I meant no disrespect on you or your family." She smiled and said, "I too am sorry for I did not realize that the worlds of the gods where so much different than ours, I do not mind the new name that has been giving me by you.

I said, "good but that is my name for you it does not replace your other names so only I will call you by that name ok?"

She smiled and said, "I like that."

About that time a boy of about eight ran up and hit the dirt so hard I think there couldn't be any skin left on his arms, when I ask what was the matter? He started talking so fast and yet I could tell a lots of the words were apologies for talking in such a manner, when he got done and Anna repeated everything it turned out not everyone could hear us.

I said to Anna, "did you have some helpers in mind that you wanted?" She looked at the group she had come from and said "I do but I have not talked to them and don't know if they would want to do it."

I said, "Great call them over here we won't tell them that part till you are ready but we need some help now."

She called out two names, which came running like the boy did when they had landed.

I said, "Look I need one of you to go part way down the group and the other further down so you can hear when she say's something you will repeat it so that all can hear." Anna told them their jobs and away they ran I told Anna to tell the boy to go back to his parents and let us know if there are any more problems. She started again and this time I heard her name where it belonged when she finished she started looking at me so I went on, "If you have problems she is the one that will arrange the time for me to hear you, if you have problems with any of the ones I have chosen, then come to me and I will deal with it myself, and yes I have chosen others." When I was done and the sound faded from the buildings I said, to Anna, "call back your friends they can stay by your side for now but the group doesn't need to be in on what is next." She called them back and they knelt just behind and to each side of Anna like book ends, when she looked back at me I turned and said, "Now for you two I am sorry I made you wait so long before I solved this problem, ok old man what is this beating about?" The old man just looked at me then at Anna back to me but saying nothing, I was getting feed up with just standing here, so I waved my hand in a circle motion you know the universal sign of get on with it, I guess Anna seen it so she barked "now old man!" She made me jump the old man I thought was going to fly he jumped so high, I laughed at her and him, but he started talking and so did Anna at first it was hard to follow both voices but I quickly was able to bleed one out and focus on her voice. The just of it was that the solder took something and when the old man said something the solder took offence and started beating the old man. I bent down on my legs so I was close to him and said, "so did you deserve it or not?" I was surprised to hear Anna had moved up close to and used the same volume and feeling as I did. The old man looked up just a little till he could see where I was then his head went down, he replied in a soft voice "I might have." I stood up and turned back to the commander and while I was saying "who are you?" When he replied he called himself captain of yeti, yeti, yeti. I said, "Ok captain tell me your side of the story. He looked back shocked why I don't know ether he wasn't used to someone listening to him or someone asking him to justify himself. I waited for a minute before looking to Anna who barked "now captain!" He was used to being barked at so he didn't jump just looked at Anna with narrow eye's I finally said, "So if you won't tell your side then you must be admitting fault, I reached and pulled out my sword."

Anna moved back the Captain tried to become the dirt but he said "I do not take orders from women; I looked down on him trying my best to look like a mountain when I said, "How dare you call me a woman I should take your life just for that alone." He looked at me then at Anna then back to me.

I was raising my sword when he said, "I didn't mean you my lord I meant the woman," pointing at Anna.

Are you def I shouted I said, "this here is no woman right now she is my voice and ear's so if I see fit to use her for this purpose then who are you to tell me I am wrong because of the vessel in which my voice comes from can't you with your own ears hear me speaking the words that you yourself are unworthy to hear direct like she can."

I looked up over his head and said to the other solders "so who out there is going to speak to my voice and to my ears when your captain is no more?" I stood looking at all the soldiers who was now calculating if it would be wise to show that you wanted his job or not at this time, I could see a couple of hands start to move when The Captain said in a very shaky voice "that he meant no disrespect and please forgive his dishonor," he said a few other things and I let him go on for quite awhile before I held up a hand then turning said to Anna "so do you forgive him?" She was shocked she looked behind her before pointing a finger to herself and saying "me?"

I said, "of course you it wasn't really me he was dishonoring but you."

She said "yes" then I turned back to the captain and said "ok we can go on but do not think I will over look this again." I kept going on now again "why were you kicking an old man plus going to kill an unarmed one?" I was not getting calm on the contrary I was getting down right upset, I caught myself and stopped talking walking in a small circle before stopping in front of the captain again, I looked over to Anna who was also scared of my rant so I said in a soft even tone "has he said something yet?"

She said, "no my lord" than looking at the captain she gave him a big break by adding he has not answered your question yet my lord, she bent to her knees and bowed. I looked back to the captain and held my gaze on him. The men near him moved away as far as they could. He looked around to see he was alone so he got his courage up and said, "I am a captain of the army of the impearl lord, All is his to be used by his army, and it is an honor to give to the impearl army, and I was teaching that peasant over there to show respect." I started laughing out loud and hard. When I stopped I could tell his courage was gone again.

I said this time with a big smile "so which one did you teach him honor, or respect?" I bent over till I was almost face to face and said well? He said in a whisper "I don't know?"

I turned around to the old man and said, "old man what did you learn: Honor or respect?" I looked at Anna who was busy shaking her head this girl is bright; before he could answer I turned back and said in a calm voice "it looks like your teaching method sucks for he learned nothing but that you were going to kill him. So captain how would you like me to teach you with my boot, or my sword?"

Chapter 2

I turned to Anna and said, "What time do you guys have supper around here?"

She was confused and it showed on her face, when she answered it was in her voice too, plus she was unsure whether it was the right answer to the question; "we normally would have started preparing about an hour ago."

I looked back to the captain and said, "I think we have held up these people long enough don't you? And if we let them go start dinner one of these nice folks might invite us to dine with them." The captain just looked blank, I had made too many turns for him to keep up with and now He didn't have a clue what to say or do, but finally nodded so I turned to Anna again and ask, "Who is in charge here?"

She laughed and said "you are." I smiled but repeated who is the village leader? She said that would be my father he is the town Elder.

Ok she was now having fun but I didn't need it right now so I said, "do you want to show me who the town elder is or do I need to ask someone else?"

She sobered right up and said "please forgive me I didn't mean any insult I do not know why I took light but please punish me as you see fit I was out of line."

I stopped her by holding up my hands when she had stop talking I turned both hands over palms up, raised them a little and said "well?"

She turned and pointed, yes it was the same old man on the ground looking at us as was everyone else but when I looked around her to see the whole group their eye shot to the ground. I had let the captain work his way backwards down the road a bit as we were talking, I said, "come on captain let's go!" I grabbed a handful of uniform and took three steps back in front of the old man, when I got there I let go and stepped aside but said, "go ahead captain it is your turn now." He looked at the old man then at me, then at Anna, a couple of trees, a rock, I think he even watched an ant walk passed. I moved half a step forward because I got bored with this and crossed my arms over my chest doing my best imitation of my mom. He jump when I started moving but when he looked up his mood hadn't improve but he got the idea, I wasn't going to let this take all night so he got on his knees very slowly like the way you'd move not to startle a wild animal, then straighten his back so he was talking down to the old man but he said, "I will forgive your actions for today so you are all free to go about your business." He looked over to me to see if he had hit a nerve or something but I didn't care how he said it, I just wanted it said. I think he could see that because he slumped forward and down. The old man started to say something but before he did I cleared me throat and when he looked my way I gave him my best I will kill you stare and shook my head he shut his mouth. I got a great big smile on my face and took the other half step so I was standing next to both of them I reached down and picked both of them up by their arms (which took everything I had because neither one wanted to stand) when they did I said, "ok, Elder if you could get your people dismissed then find a place where we could set down I think that the three of us need to talk, they both looked at Anna, I looked to and said, "I wouldn't be doing much talking without her would I; so now she is me!"

They stood there for a minute before the old man said "as you wish my lord it shall be."

I seen movement out of the corner of my eye so I said, "sirs, please excuse me a minute I have to see someone else right now so don't run off." The last part I said looking at the captain. I walked off not looking back just knowing Anna would come with me. What I seen was the lady, whose charges I have been pulling for helpers all day. She was gathering her charges and getting ready to leave, I walk straight up to her bowing I said, "I want to thank you for the fine women who you have in your care." I looked up to realize I should be looking down because they were laying flat on the ground. I looked to see Anna who was there but breathing hard (I guess I assumed too much but she caught up because she didn't miss a word). I looked at her then at the women on the ground I had to do it a couple of times before she caught on she said in a whisper her name I shrugged she just nodded. I said, "Please rise." The women looked at Anna then at me; Anna bent over and gave her a hand to get her to her knees.

I said, "I wanted you to know you have done a good job teaching your young women honor in their jobs and calling.

The women bowed her head when Anna had finished talking then she spoke she said, "Forgive me my Lord for not knowing but would you tell an unworthy servant what you are the god of?"

I said without thinking or my answer might have been different, "honor and fighting!"

She said, "I do not understand my lord."

I said, "I will take time to teach you before I go if possible."

She bowed again and said, "I am humbly your grateful servant my lord."

I said, "I will need a couple more of your charges before I am done, Anna will get with you later on who I will need."

She didn't even look up when she said. "It would be an honor for whoever you chose, even myself if my lord wishes."

I bowed again and said, "thank you, now I have other work to do tonight, then I still have to find a place to sleep." Anna stop short on the translation I didn't know how I knew but it just stopped to sharply so I looked at her she had that wide eyed look again, like I had just done the unthinkable again. When she looked at me she bowed and finished now the old woman look surprised.

She said, "My lord is there a problem with the temple grounds we will fix any problem that my master has with the bed that is prepared for you there."

I bowed "there is no problem I would be honored to stay there, but it is not an honorable thing to come and stay without being invited, a wife invites her husband every day after a hard day's work by greeting him at the door does she not? A husband invites his wife to come and set with him in the evening hours, this is honor given and shared. I then cannot or will not throw my honor by the wayside nor would I take away the chance for you to grow your honor by sharing that which you are in charge of. I realized that Anna was yelling again and the echoing had returned, when I get like this I see my father face as he would recite one of those life lessons, he would call them so I was surprised when I looked around to see what looked to be the whole town around me listening this included the solders mixed in with the people. The people were on their knees and when I looked around it was like a wave in the bleachers of a stadium as all the heads bowed to the ground. When I got back to the woman I started with I bowed and said again "it will be my honor to stay where you have prepared a place for me to rest my head."

She said quietly "the honor is mine, my lord and dinner will be ready when you are."

I thanked her again worked my way through the crowd and found the old man. He bowed as I approached I said, "Ok where to Elder?"

"My places if it is ok with you my lord," he replied.

I said, "Lead the way then," and we were off, but this time I checked to be sure Anna was in tow.

Chapter 3

We arrived at the Elders house he walked right up to the door, slide it opened and walked in, slipping off his shoes at the step before walking on in I stopped at the door, when the captain seen me stop he did to, Anna bringing up the rear actually ran into the captain when she apologized it got the Elders attention so that he turned around to look to see what was going on. When he looked back his face changed to horror and ran back to the step and fell to his knees and face saying "I am sorry, I didn't mean no disrespect, but please come in and make my house your home."

I said, "thank you," so did the captain, I noticed Anna bowed before entering. I turned set on the step and began untying my shoes (hiking boots aren't made to come off easily). I pulled the first off before I noticed the shadow's that was over me, I looked up to find all three were looking at my shoes, I spoke before they noticed I was looking and said "you like my shoes?" They all jumped which made me laugh, I said "if you would like to look at them go ahead." I finished pulling my other boot off and handed it to the

Elder who had waited too long before trying to pick up the first one. They turned them over and stroked the sides but I stopped them from putting their hands inside, then took them back and set them on the ground besides each other, before the captain ask, "what kind of animal has that kind of skin, and where can I hunt him?"

I said, "Sorry Captain that will have to wait till another time."

He bowed his head and said, "Yes my lord at your leisure." I got up from the step and said "Elder I think this is not the place you had in mind to set so if you please."

He got to his feet and said, "Yes my lord if you would follow me please."

And we were off again. He took us to a room with a short table, and some cushions on the floor. Stepping inside the room he stood aside for us to pass then we stared at each other for a moment till I caught on he was waiting on me I said, "Elder this is your house so please be seated as you normally would." He looked like a dear in headlights but moved over and set down I followed and found a set on the end of the table facing the door, the captain set across from the elder. When we all got comfortable I said "Ok Captain, tell us a little about you?"

He started like any old movie "I am so and so son of such and such ect, ect," I did find out his father and his father's father was captains of the Imperial guard and that one day he wants to be (and expected to be) Captain of the Imperial guard as well. He is currently assigned to the young crown prince who when he takes over for his dad he then will become the captain of the Imperial guard. He went on talking for a while I let him go on and on, the more he talked the more confidence he got the more he talked. I listened tell he ran out of things to say.

I said, "Very good, so elder now it is your turn to tell us about you."

He also started by going I am the son of and so forth, what I got was he was the son of every elder to oversee this town, that it was his family that founded this town from emperor so and so, I quit trying to remember names hours ago. Then came a knock on the door, it slide just a little opened and a soft voice came In "I have fix some tea for you and your guest my husband." The elder looked at us and ask, "Would like something to drink?" we both nodded, he then answered her saying "yes you may enter and serve us."

I ask, "Is this your wife?"

He looked unsure for a moment then said "yes."

Then I said, "If you would excuse me I must do something," without waiting for his permission I got up and walked to the door as it was sliding open to reveal a very beautiful woman on her knees with a tray of cups and saucers. She looked up then froze putting her face down. I knelt down so I was facing her then putting my forehead to the ground as I had seen them all do. Before saying, "I am honored to meet you for I have seen with my own eyes the care you have given this land, and this house. I have seen you treat everything that is yours with honor and respect, the gods of this place must be blessed for the care and sacrifice that you have given, I also looked forward to meeting all of your children for I have meet Anna so I know you have taught your children well, so bring them to me when covenant for you before I leave this village, I also feel blessed that our shoes have not let the dust fall, that you are here to serve us with this tea, so I take this time to show my honor for you." I bowed again then got up without another word and went back to my seat. After I set down I looked to the elder and said, to him "sir I hope you know how blessed you have been to be given a wife of such worth, I hope that you know that your rise or fall will depend on the honor with which you treat her."

When I finished I just sat there looking at him, then that voice again "may I serve now my lord?" He shook his head, "Yes," she started to crawl into the room on her knees to serve us then he said something else that Anna didn't translate till I looked around at her when she said he said. "I should be helping her." I looked back to him who was looking daggers at her and I said, "you are right" and I stood up again everyone froze in place I walked back to the woman who again was laying face down, I reached down and gently pulled up on her elbow till she looked up, I told Anna tell her to come with me. I finally had to look over to the elder and tell him the same thing. I got her to her feet but her head never came up I lead her to my spot on the floor where I set her down then I walked over to the tray and picked it up. Anna right away tried to take the tray saying "this is not proper."

I said, "you are my voice which means you are a part of me when we are together, the lord of this house has said to serve tea and serve tea I will for my honor is at stake here but my voice don't serve tea my hands do so as my voice you need to tell them what I am saying while I serve them tea!"

He started shouting before I made the table first at Anna then at me then the room and his wife. When he slowed down Anna started translating, the jest of it was he wasn't having it and god or not I was not going to tell him what to do. When Anna had finished I had made the table I set the tray down bowed to the elder then turned and without a word left. I was putting my boots back on when Anna came running up to me and ask "where are you going?"

I said, "I will not be where there is no honor or a chance of teaching honor so I will go because I am not wanted here, and you do have a chose if you want I will chose another to be my voice but I will not take my voice from you." I finished tying my shoes and stood, when I turned around all of them were standing there, I said to Anna, "you would honor me if you would tell them what I told you," I turned to face the captain bowed and said "I hope to get a chance to talk to you before you go." I turned around opened the door and left.

When I got to the road I turned the opposite way then we had come earlier. I walked till I came to the edge of town. I was looking out over plowed field with a tree line down the road about a quarter mile. I was thinking now what do I do? There beside the road were three rocks two were flat one round, so I stacked them on top of each others to make a small tower then to make things even I looked around till I found three more rocks that looked the same and stacked them on the other side of the road. Looking at them both I said, "I have seen this in a book somewhere before, it marks a temple or someplace sacred," then I knelt beside one of the stone towers and looked up into the sky and said out loud "lord what am I suppose to do now? I need help because I don't have a clue what you want from me, can I go home now?" I waited but here I stayed. I got to my feet turned around and I had a very sober crowd in front of me, in front of them all was Anna, she walked up to me and said, "I am your voice and any help I can give is always yours." After a pause she continued "we are sorry for our action and hope you can forgive us for that which we did."

I said, "I don't know I have come to teach this town at this time about honor, I don't see a lot of people ready to learn except maybe those that don't need much of a lesson."

She said, "I don't understand but I will listen till I do so will you come back to the house and start over my father ask this himself."

I said, "He won't like the lessons I believe." She shrugged. Then the crowd parted like the Red Sea and coming through the crowd was Anna's mother, she walked up to me took my arm and gently led the way back to the house.

When we were back at the table fresh hot tea and apologies done with (I did not apologies). I started again I took off the Captains sword putting it on the table then I ask the captain "what is this sword good for?"

The Captain said, "That sword protects the royal family and their subjects from people who have a will to do them harm, it is a symbol of my honor, and of my status in the royal court." I turned to the elder, "what is this sword good for?"

The Elder responded, "It would protect the village from bandits who steal our crops, and bring meat and food for the village.

I said to both "you are wrong! This sword does nothing it will cut only if I use it to, it will protect only if I use it, and it will kill only if I kill. So what is this sword good or bad?" They looked at each other but before they could answer I went on. "This sword is neither good nor bad the knife your wife makes dinner with is good in her hands but could kill in mine. So weapons of all type are good and bad so do you know what makes it a good weapon?" They looked at each other again but this time I didn't jump in to save them.

Finally the elder said, "We do not know lord."

I then looked both in the eyes when I said, "that is because both of you are lacking this item in you. You are both low on honor and I think it is because you don't understand honor. I can see both of you need more honor in your life. That sword if wielded by a man with honor is a sword of good for the man will not let it do other than that which is honorable. A sword wielded by a man of no honor is unpredictable there for it is a sword that is bad."

The captain asked, "then how do we get honor my lord."

I replied "you do not take honor you give honor." They looked confused again so I took my cup of water and spill a little on the table then I gave each man a pair of chop sticks. And said, "Ok there is honor on the table now pick it up and put it in the cup!"

Both men looked at the water then the cup and the chop sticks before saying "it can't be done my lord."

I said, "Right it can't be done" (then I took a napkin and wiped up the water) "but soon the honor is gone."

So again both men asked, "So how do we get honor" and again

I said "wrong question. You do not get honor any more then you picked the water up and put it in the cup honor is a fragile thing that is in your soul no one can take it from you, but they can give it to you, can't be taken by force but can be earned. Fear, status, money these are not honors. These are just fears and desires, they honor you because you are Elder, but they do not give you honor, they follow you captain because you are their leader, but they are not giving you honor. So many famous men die without honor all the glory no honor. So in the next life they can't go on for no man can go without honor."

Then I took two more cups putting a little water in both, and said, "I gave you honor in your cup" then I poured some back as I said, "then you gave me back honor and has I give out honor and honor is returned I find my cup is always full. But remember if I speak harshly to one who doesn't deserve it or beat up on one that can't defend himself or watch as someone else takes advantage of another then I have spilt my honor on uncaring ground that won't give it back then I have given what no man can take. This goes for the women in our lives too. Most women have more honor than men for we give it to the ground to freely." Both men looked at Anna as she said this. "I see by the shadows on the wall that it is getting late in the day so I think this is good for now." Turning to the captain I went on "do you have a place for you and your men to bed down for the night?"

He said, "Yes they are already making camp."

Good I replied, "So elder if you will excuse me I need to go and I would like to see you off in the morning captain." Both men bowed and followed me to my shoes, then at the door I noticed both men went back inside to talk some more.

Anna followed me out I ask, "don't you sleep here" she said "no I will sleep at the temple with you for where else would a voice sleep then with its master?" She had me there.

Chapter 4

So we started the long walk up the mountain to the temple. When we started the climb I noticed the youngest maiden playing about half way up the steps, she was skipping up and down the steps and from one side of the path to the other. Anna said in a whisper "she wasn't supposed to do that."

I whispered back "why not she is still a child and fun is where you can find it."

She said "but it is unbecoming a temple maiden."

I replied and forgot to whisper "HOG WASH!"

Anna looked at me and said, "Wash what?"

I laugh "no hog wash," shaking my head I said, "Never mind." The little girl had heard us and stopped playing when she seen us looking her way she bolted up the stairs towards the temple I laughed again I guess this is their early warning system. We talked the rest of the way about whether a girl was prettier and more relaxed when she was playing or sober and what is the right way for a temple maiden to act, when we got to the gate I told Anna she was not to say anything about the girl on the steps. When Anna nodded ok we went in. We walked up to the house (the house was huge, bigger than any in the village) the women were lined up along the walk way, and of course on their knees. I stopped when we got to the woman I had talked to earlier bent down and said, "I know you are showing respect but you are temple maidens right, and if I get this right you are here to take care of the temple and care for the gods am I right?

I stopped talking and waited for an answer. She finally said "yes my lord that is right but you are the first god that as chose to visit this shrine."

I said, "how do you know is it based on the fact that you have not seen them, and yet you have all of their shrines here so why would they not visit whether they reviled themselves to you or not."

There was a long pause before she said, "I don't know."

I said, "to be honest here, I don't know why I am here, but I think that I am here to show you and this village the things I see that need to be looked at differently or like my father would tell me with honor, I have already told you I am impressed with the skill and honor you have taught these girls to do the job that is before them but I think it is important that they learn to have fun and satisfaction in doing the job itself, and one of the ways to do that is to realize that the gods you take care of are real and that they care. I am sorry I talk too much about things I believe in. Back to my first point and that is as long as I am here would you please not kneel, for if I would ask one of you something you cannot do it if you are on the ground, second it means that if you are taking care of other business you then would stop to bow to the ground as I pass so if you must then just bow and go on doing whatever you were doing, can we do that?"

She had a mental fight in her head that showed on her face then said, "we will do as my lord ask only at the temple, if we see you in town we will show proper respect to our lord."

I nodded before I said, "I can live with that, now could you all rise." She stood with head bowed, and all but two of the girls followed suit. I said, "Great now I need one more thing from you like Anna you are a leader and as such I will need you to look at me when I talk to you, so please raise your head." She shook her head no so I reached out put my finger under her chin and lifted till she was looking at me when I said "good much better. I will call you head mistress when I address you is that ok?" She nodded. I went on "good now if you would like to show me around a minute I would be honored." She bowed again this time at the waist turned and headed for the door.

We entered a large open room, doors slid opened let in sun light that bathed every corner in a soft glow, and also gave you a good view of the outside. There was a table set in the middle of the floor about three foot high just like I had set at in town. The head mistress said, "Dinner is ready when you are my lord."

I said, "Great I am starving!" I was shown to the end of the table, Anna at the other end, plates were place in front of us then food started coming in and set on the table when everything was in (I know this because it quit coming) two of the girls stayed and the head mistress stood by the side of the door that all the food came in. When I didn't start eating the head mistress said "do you want someone to feed my lord?"

I almost choked right there I said, "why would I want that?"

She responded by saying "we have heard that some lords require someone to feed them."

I said "shaking my head that sounds sick; I just was waiting on everyone else to set down to eat." This time Anna almost choked before translating it.

The head mistress looked horrified, my lord she stammered, "It is improper to share a table with one such as yourself!"

I looked down at my lap before saying "I know I am not much to look at and my manners may be rusty but I know what not to do at a table that I am a guest at."

Anna and the headmistress looked confused then she shook her head and bowed. "I am sorry my lord I didn't mean you my lord I meant us we are not worthy of setting at your table when you eat."

I didn't like where this was going and I was getting tired of everyone telling me what I should do or say and what they can or cannot do in my presents, and this was going to stop here. I said with a tone of frustration; "you mean to tell me who I can or cannot eat dinner with or set with or talk too, then my dear women I will go somewhere that I can enjoy the company I am with and they can enjoy me!"

I started to raise when Anna spoke up without translating; "my lord please we don't understand your ways, and ask for your forgiveness, we will try to do as you say but we are only doing as we have been taught," all the women in the room laid flat on the ground with Anna repeating this over and over with the other also saying "forgive us."

I set back down the truth was, where was I going to go, I didn't know instead I said, "ok, but you are wrong I am a guest here and this is your table, but let's try this while I am here we are family, we eat together, we set together and we can talk freely to each other, I cannot understand your conversations without Anna translating, but I will learn some words and phrases. I will play head of house will I am here and yes I understand these changes only apply to the temple grounds. Please take a moment to talk to all the girls and whoever lives here and if this is ok then call the girls, priests, gardeners whoever to dinner and let's eat!" An hour later they started filing in. I wouldn't let them warm up dinner I said "this is the way it is served if you wanted it warm you should have been on time. I told them that was a saying from my mom" (if some of them where surprised that a god had a mom none showed it);

I didn't tell them if you were an hour late there was no food because she had thrown it out. I ask;" Anna does everyone understand now?" She shook her head as she was saying "I don't understand my lord."

I said, "ok little step will be ok." They waited till I filled my plate and then I had to tell Anna that I would wait for them to fill theirs. When I was done I bowed my head and said a little prayer. "Lord please bless this house, the people that reside here, and this food amen." They all clap their hands and said something I didn't understand then looked at me I know this from traveling so I took the first bite, then another then said ok let's eat. Some of the girls tried a bite or two to see if it was a trick or something, but when they didn't get into trouble finally the whole group started eating. About half way through dinner I ask Anna to ask the girl on my right to tell me her name and a little bit about herself. I hoped Anna wasn't to hungry that night because with the wanting to bow or stand or not talk dinner took three hours before we got through, I listened to everyone even if I didn't understand them but I watched them as they talked, by the end there was even other conversations going on at the same time quietly of course. When they were all done I ask if I could be shown to my room because it had been a long day for me. The girls all moved to the end of the room that was opposite me, the headmistress said, "this way my lord." And lead me down a short hallway slide another door open, bowed on her knees on the other side and said "this is your room my lord if it doesn't meet your lords' approval please let us fix it for you. And your bath is run when you are ready."

I said, "That sounds good let me get a change of cloth and I will take it now." The rest of the evening went off without a hitch that is until I got back to my room to find I could have housed a large family inside and would have had room to spare. There was nothing in the room except a sleeping mat in the middle of the room. There was a knock and I said, "come in" Anna slid a door on the end of the room open without entering she said, "I will be here you will only have to speak for me to hear you and do your biding."

I said "good night," then set out to slide open all the doors to find out where they went. Most opened outside but two were rooms (one was Anna's) and the other was a smaller room about the size of a big walk-in closet, it felt more comfortable so I moved in there. In the morning I woke up before the sun, putting on my jeans and an old t-shirt, I walked quietly through the house till I was outside again, starting my stretching for my morning exercises. I slowly walked around the temple grounds when I came up to a shine I bowed my deepest bow and said "good morning and thank you for letting me stay here with you," I repeated this over and over at every shine box I could see. I did see one shine that was at the edge of the tree line that had vines growing on it, grass growing right up to the stone I said, to this one as I took a minute to pull the vines off; "it looks like you have been neglected." I bowed and said "I apologize I am sure they just got busy with their other duties and didn't mean for this to happen to you." When I got done I finished my tour of the grounds then ran a lap or two before going down the stairs than turning around when I got to the bottom and ran back up, those stairs were longer this morning then I remember them from last night. I made my way to the back again to do my daily sword practice, surprising two of the girls when I came around the building when I was done; they fell to the ground I said "now girls remember the rules." They didn't understand me Anna wasn't there so I put my finger under their chin one at a time till they were standing, then handing them their brooms after making a few swipes with both of them before giving them up. When they started on their own I went on. At the door there appeared to be a pile of food (I didn't check it out), but once Inside I made it to where I had taken the bath the night before and washed off again. In my room, I put on my last clean pair of clothes, I folded the dirty ones, leaving them in a corner, and told myself I will have to figure out how to clean those, because I am sure there isn't any laundry mats here... I said, "Anna are you ready to go?"

The door slid open to reveal Anna in a long white kimono, on her knees, head bowed, when she looked up she said, "As you wish my lord." I walked over and put my hand down to help her up. She looked at the hand then at me before,

I said, "Let me help you up." She finally took my hand and stood; when she did I couldn't help myself I gave a little whistle walking around her I said, "You are one beautiful woman!"

She bowed" I am please you think so my lord."

"Well I do indeed so let's get going" I finished.

When we walked in the big room the head mistress meet us bowed and said "breakfast is ready at your leisure my lord."

I said "breakfast?"

She nodded "yes, didn't you see all the food that the villagers brought to honor you when you came in this morning?"

Anna spoke, "then you went out master without me?"

I looked at her and shrugged "just morning exercises." We followed the head mistress to the same table we ate at last night. I ask "will the girls be joining us this morning or are they all ready gone?"

She bowed really deep this time has she said, "I am sorry my lord many had their duties to get too so most have already eaten and gone."
 I smiled and said "no problem I will look forward to see them this evening then."

Chapter 5

The Captain and the Elder meet us at the stairs when we came down I was happy to see both were still talking. I said, "good morning" and bowed. They did the same, I said, "captain, I see you have a new friend." The captain nodded; "yes my lord" was his reply. "Good! Are you ready to go then?" I said as I walked up and put my arm around him and the Elder and started walking to the main road and the edge of town. I had thought about what I wanted to do, (or how to handle this meeting this morning); it didn't come to me till this morning run. So when we came to the village edge I already had a stick set aside. I let go of the two men picked up the stick then digging it in the ground I made a line from one of the stones I had stacked earlier to the other then I made a big box on the outside of the line, then, drawing another box on the village side with a small box connected to the side of it. I put the stick back by the wall where I had picked it up from, then walking back to the two men, I said to the captain, "If you would follow me, please."

I lead the captain to the box outside of the line then waved for him to step in. When he had done that I walked over to Anna, took her arm and lead her to the little box having her step into that box, then I stepped into the big box on the village side facing the captain I bowed deep before saying; "Captain it has been a honor to meet and talk to you, I have a gift for you to begin with." I reached into my pocket pulling out an old police whistle, which I gave to him. He took it with reverence looking at it as he turned it over and over. "When someone from the army wishes to enter the village you will step into that box and blow the whistle three times, wait then do it again; till the Elder, Anna, or I come to stand in this box. If any man with a weapon crosses that line without first being given permission I will take it they are sacrificing their life to me and I will take it; do you understand, captain?"

He nodded "yes."

"Good! I went on, these boxes are places of truth and honor any man women or child that sets foot in these boxes will speak only truth with the thought of the honor of whoever is standing in the other box.

There is no rank, gender, age, or birth right. You, as a man, can talk as an equal to a god as long as you are in the boxes, and when you leave only with a new understanding of both parties and a friend ship to be built on too. Captain, we are now friends in or out of the boxes, I hope you have learned how to regain your honor and live a full life; I need you to deliver a message for me. Everything from this line is now under my protection, it is mine now. Do you have anything to say while we are in the box?"

He bowed then said, "I, too am honored to be able to call you friend, I wish to give you thanks for teaching me, and I swear I will do as you have taught me."

I said when he had finished, "ok, captain, I wish you well and a safe journey." With that I stepped out of the box turned to Anna and said "be sure everyone knows what the boxes are for, and that they are for all to use, I am going for a walk." The crowd parted for me as I walked through them to no place special. I walked back to the temple remembering my morning stretch, I searched around till I found the gardening shed where I picked up a hand rake, some shears, and a small spade then headed for the shrine that was being over grown with weeds.

I was just getting done with the shrine when I saw Anna and the head mistress coming my way, nether looked happy, I stood up, bowed to the shine, and said out loud, "There; much better, I hope you feel better too!" I turned as the head mistress got there so I bowed again but to her and said, "thank you for giving me this honor to clean this shrine I will put away the tools now." I straightened up and walked back to the tool shed stopping long enough on the way to wash the dirt off. When I came out of the shed I almost knocked Anna down. She had been running to catch up; I smiled to see she had out run the head mistress. I told her I was sorry and we both laughed, until the head mistress got there. Anna explained that when she had finished she could not find me, when she got up to the temple, no one had seen me so all of the maidens are out searching for me now, then Anna began to cry. I felt bad so I said, "I am right here and I didn't mean to make you sad, but why are you crying?"

She finally said, "I was afraid you had left us; "I could see what looked like tears in the head mistress eye's and her head moving up and down out of the corner of my eye. I stepped over and hugged Anna for a second then stepped back before explaining "Look, I don't know why I am here or when I will go but I will someday go.

I don't want to leave sadness when I do so, when that time comes, remember the things that I have taught, not the sorrow of my leaving." I stepped over to the head mistress giving her a hug too, for she indeed, was crying as well. We went back down the mountain to the village where I got to spend the rest of the day listening to every person in the village in the box. I missed lunch so when dinner came I was starving; Anna told them all that it was time to go home for the evening. I stopped Anna before she could leave, and then waited for the crowd to leave before putting her in the other box. I said, "Anna, I am not a god I am a man from your future I have come, I think; to help, the only life lesson I know is honor and I am very good at hand weapon fighting. I feel that you needed to know the truth, when I was brought here to your time and the first thing I saw was a dispute with no honor the rest has been one response to an action to another response to a different action; you get the idea. I am afraid I will offend someone because I do not know the customs or the way life is now," she was looking at me intently, I didn't know what I expected but I needed to tell her, or someone.

She smiled then bowed before looking me in the eye's and "saying you may not believe you are a god. Yet you just said you come from my future, you say you don't know why you are here and yet you have saved this village and my father from death. You are afraid you are going to offend us by your action and yet gods themselves are strange and expected to be for we all know your world is not ours. I will do my best to help you in doing your work here for as long as you are here." She bowed then stepped out of the box, I followed her movements and we went to the temple but if I thought my day was through,

I was wrong. When we got to the temple we were surrounded by the maidens asking questions, I heard Anna tell them things like, "no, he didn't go, Yes, he was cleaning a shrine, no he isn't mad at whoever didn't take care of it," so on and so on I walked on.

Chapter   6

There was a man dressed differently than any I had seen so far, I thought maybe a priest for I haven't seen one of them, but he waved so I went over to him, when I got close he said, (and I understood him), "welcome to our village we have been waiting a long time for you to arrive." He bowed then stood up and reached out a hand for a hand shake. I took it and he smiled and said, "I wasn't for sure that was right, we were told by the wondering god of the west that is how you great friends."

I smiled then said, "I give but who are you and how do I understand you?"

He looked shocked for a moment then again bowed and laughed," so sorry I did skip that part didn't I? We are the gods of this Temple, mountain, and village. And as gods our selves we can understand and speak any language that is spoken to us."

I said, "Ok, who is "we then?"

He laughed, and then said, "Let's go see them, for yourself."

Anna walked up to me at that time and said, "You ok master?"

I looked at her then at him before he said, "she cannot see me or hear me either, unless I will it and I won't." Before you ask "she cannot go where we are going."

I turned to face Anna and said please go in and have dinner tell the girls I am sorry but I (I stumbled for the right words before saying), I have to meet with some new friends."

The guy laughed hard then said, "I like you already." He held out his hand again I took it as a door appeared we stepped through to a world that was full, yet roomy white yet full of color to a group of people different sizes and shapes. All were standing except one who was rolling on the floor laughing his head off to the annoyance of all, he ran into (and I think he hit everyone but me) when he settled down some he said between short burst of laugher," so much for the "not a god" image you just disappeared into a shrine in front of all of the temple maidens! Let's see her cover that up!" He started laughing and rolling again.

The god that had led me here said, "That is the god of mirth and tricksters; He likes a good joke." He led me around the group introducing me around to the other gods; the god of the mountain was big and had a big voice. The god of the trees was, I think green talked slow, but was very beautiful, and, I couldn't tell male or female, we went around I think there is a god for everything, most are stuck to this spot but some can wonder, like the one the trickster said, let her cover that up, is the god to protect gods, who knew right. Then we came to the end when he said, "there is one more who wishes to see you," from the back came a soft looking and spoken god that always seems to be changing but, slowly, so you could see the changes and yet she was beautiful in all her changes. She stepped forward and bowed, no one else bowed but I bowed back.

She said in a soft bubbling voice, "I thank you for your care and respect given at my shine today. So many have passed me by but you took the time, and then came back as you said you would. I am deeply honored to meet you god of honor." She stood and went back to behind the group.

I looked at my host, and he shrugged "She is the god of water and streams; she goes where she wants to, for she is stronger than most here."

I said with a smile, "ok and you are?"

He smiled, "we are kindred spirits, my friend for I am the god of knowledge and information." He went on, "we have some information for you now you no longer need the medallion around your neck to travel time, for you have grown in your powers quite fast for being new at it, that medallion is your tie to this time only when you get ready to go just take the medallion off giving it to someone you trust to give it back when the time comes and you then can leave but once you left, you cannot return to this time."

"How do I travel in time," I said, "and when did I become the god of honor?"

He winked as he said, "the minute you said that oath you became a god and the people have named you the god of honor and truth. You just need to picture where you want to go and you will go there. You also will find you can hear voices and or sounds that is said or done in your honor no matter where or when they are done, in this world, so don't forget to listen." I thanked him and then I talked to all of them most just wanted to know about my time and world.

When I returned to the world I had left it was dark but one lit lantern and a maiden set by the shrine sleeping, I picked her up and the lantern then headed for the house and a long awaited dinner.

Three weeks went by, and I finally got into a routine, in the morning saying hello to the shrines, my run then sword practice, two or three hours in the box, then the rest of my free time going out into the country side to visit the people who lived out there. Yes in fact I was getting really bored. I wanted to go home but I was waiting for something I just didn't know what.

Chapter 7

Then it happened, one morning before the box. I was coming down the steps from the temple when it started, the buzzing in my head. It set my teeth on edge, then I recognized it, it was the whistle, I had given the Captain. I ran to the edge of the village, he wasn't there so where was he? Then it hit me if he wasn't here and he was blowing the whistle then my friend was in trouble, and that was all I needed to know. I could see Anna coming down the road so I yelled to her to "hurry up! We got to go!"

She didn't even blink she ran up to me and said, "Where are we going?"

I held her by the shoulders and said, "I don't know but I do know this is going to be new for you but I can't do it on my own so keep your wits about you and be careful."

She nodded, "yes."

"Ok! I said, as I pulled her close, "hold on then."

I thought about the Captains face and him blowing that whistle, and then it was breaking my ear drums. I yelled Anna, "Tell him to stop!"

When it got quiet I looked around. We were in a large room or would be but it was cut in half by a screen that let you see shadows of who was on the other side, five of us were on this side, besides Anna and myself The Captain was lying face down on the floor with the whistle in his mouth, two men standing over him with swords drawn, ready to cut his head off, or so it looked to me. I said, "Hi, Captain you don't look so good." He shrugged but didn't say anything then a voice came from the other side of the screen; he yelled "it is a demon, kill him!" That was my cue: I jumped over the captain bringing my sword up, as they brought theirs down, I took a quick stock of the two guards, one was young and one was older, the younger's feet were wrong and his grip off not by much but enough, the older one didn't make those mistakes so with that I said in my mind. "Ok the young one it is." I jumped up and kicked the older one in the chest as hard as I could with that armor on I was hoping he would be off balance, he stumbled backwards and fell that was all I was going to get, so I turned to attack the young one. I wasn't playing fair or even using my sword I pushed him with my body and my sword till he had his sword up against his own chest then changing hands I put all my power into a right hook that caught him under the chin I think I broke all my fingers because his chin was made of stone, but lucky for me it was made of glass too because his eyes rolled up and he went down. I didn't wait for him to hit the ground before turning and walking back to the older guy. He was just getting to his feet and stopped for a moment to watch his friend hit the dirt, he looked up to see me step over the Captain and heading his way so he set his feet and waited I yelled to Anna "tell the Captain to get out of the middle of the floor!" I could see from the corner of my eye the captain start crawling backwards towards where I had heard Anna's voice came from. I meet the other guard with our swords, and the fight was on, it didn't take long before I knew this guy was as good as or better than me, and he know the same about me, this was going to be a fight of mistakes, the first one to make a mistake loses his life. I wasn't going to take his if I could help it, but I may not have a choice and I had no doubt about the fact he would take mine. This fight was dragging on I could see him getting tired but so was I then there it was, the mistake I was looking for he went high leaving his body open, he knew it, too, but before he could recover I stabbed him in the stomach I went all the way through, I just hope I didn't hit anything vital. He faulted when he did I knocked his sword out to his side and placed the tip of mine at his throat. He let his sword drop but he didn't look to me but at the screen.

I found I had to look too, then I heard that voice again, "kill him, he has failed."The man before me closed his eyes waiting to die. I put my sword back in its scabbard as I said, "horse pucky, I will." The man opened his eyes and looked at Anna then at me before sliding to the ground. He was bleeding pretty badly but I was glad to see it was all bright red, which was a good sign. I bent the man forward and he moaned with the pain I said I was sorry but this needed taking care of or he would bleed to death. I pulled a little knife I had in my belt and cut the fabric from around the wound, the nice thing about a small bladed sword is it leaves a small wound. I pushed the guy as easy as I could back and did the same for the front, then I stood up turning to Anna I said, "Tell

the Captain to explain who I am while I am g
and I will be right back. Don't let him forget
tell them who you are, too." With that I made a
mental picture and was gone. When I got back the
Captain was still talking, Anna started to translate
and I told her "I was ok with not going over it
again if the subject changed then let me know." I
knelt down to the guard on the floor, pulled up my
emergency kit (bag really, mom said if you play
with knives you need a bigger kit) I rolled the
guard forward till I could see the hole, took my
fingers pinching the two sides together, then
placing a couple of butterfly bandages on it to
hold it shut put some antibiotic cream around the
outside with a little pain killer, then a big gauze
pad held down with tape when I rolled him back,
again saying "I was sorry but, I have to stop the
bleeding." I started to do the same on the front
when he asked me "why?" I have heard that so
much that I knew what he said before Anna told
me, I said, "you are a master and a man of honor.
I am also a man of honor. We men of honor know
that we must protect those who cannot protect
themselves, and to honor them that do good in this
world, plus we who fight honor those we fight

with our best then when it is over we take care of the wounded and the dead so that when we meet our relatives in the hereafter, we can do so with or heads up high, for those that live like us we then can meet as friends or as honored foes on the battle field. I am not your enemy so I count you has friend. Pointing a finger over my head to the wall, I count him as friend too, his technique is good but needs a lot more practice."

He laugh then grabbed his side before saying, "I have been telling him the same thing myself." He bobbed a head and said "you have a friend here too." I finished what I was doing then stood up taking my sword out I cut down one of the banners ask Anna to hold one corner while I held the other, then cut it into one long ribbon then two. I wrapped the ribbon around the guard, said this is going to hurt and cinched it up to hold both pads in place then tied a knot in it.

"There", I said, "now rest here, I will be back before I go, and could you talk to your friend over there? I see him beginning to move and I do not want to kill him if I don't have to." Anna was pulling on my sleeve and pointing to the curtain even while she was translating for me, so I turned as she said, "that is the crown prince he has called for his priest to expel you."

Right on cue the priest arrived nine to be exact the prince told them to get rid of the demon. One of the priests replied, "no problem, my lord, for our god is greater and at your bidding."

That just seemed to rub me the wrong way why would a god be at his bidding; shouldn't a god be for all the people not just for the privileged ones with no honor? So if it has to be, a show down then it has to be, then what! I don't want to fight, so in any conflict there needs to be understanding. So, I know just the man, or god, to enlighten me and I think I will take a guest.

I said, "Anna, which one is the head priest?" She pointed to the one that had spoken. All the priest were chanting, making hand gestures, and waving what looked to be pom-poms I told Anna, "be safe, I will be back," then turning my head,

I said, "Hey, buddy, can you watch that kit for me till I return?"

He said, "with my remaining life if need be!"

I said, "Don't go that far but thanks." I know I had to be giving them a funny look but it wasn't as funny as the look of the head priest when I walked up to him and said, "Let's go meet your god." With that said, I pictured white scenery and a face of a god and there he was smiling.

He said, "I knew you would be back, but not so soon and I see you have brought a guest with you."

I said, "Yes, he is a priest who promised his god would banish me; I don't know what I have done so I came to you so you could tell me about him and what I must do now." His smile vanished. "His god is not a he, his god is a she, and she is not a minor god like us, she is a major god who protects the royal family; sorry that's wrong she protects royal families no matter where they are from. She can be unpredictable if I were you I would go back to your world and hope she doesn't get involved.

I noticed I have not heard a word from the priest so I turned around looking down, I said, "What got you so quiet now."

The god of knowledge said," he now can understand us remember?"

I smiled and said, "OH, I forgot."

Before I could say anything to the wide eye priest the god of knowledge said, "Oops! Too late, here she comes."

I looked in the direction he was looking and it looked like storm clouds covering the whole land, as far as I could see and it was defiantly coming to us. When it arrived I bowed, but noticed I bowed alone the other god was gone. I stayed bowed saying nothing till a sweet voice vibrated the landscape.

"So, you are the god of honor who we have been watching with great satisfaction of your good deeds please rise and walk with me.

I stood up then waved a hand to the back of me and said, "I have brought you a gift my Lady."

She looked back over my shoulder and said with thunder coming from around her, "I see you have brought me one who has been taking my name and used it for his own profit, I thank you for this gift." Then two figures came from the storm shadows and grabbed the man then disappeared. The sweet voice came back I shall talk with him later when you get back tell them I said, "Jonathan will now be my head priest and to remember I do listen."

I said, "Jonathan my Lady?"

"Yes," she said, "and please, call me Elizabeth when we are together."

I stammered "Elizabeth?"

You repeat names a lot don't you?

I said, "I am sorry my, ha, Elizabeth."

She laughed, "ok now what did you won't from me?"

I said, "not to fight I would like your permission to show the crown prince about having honor."

She stopped walking turned to look at me before saying "I will allow it but I will not give you aid if you need it."

I said "that is good for if I used help I think the lesson will be lost."

She laughed again then started walking and said, "I think you need to return now and thank you for the gift, I shall return the favor one day."

I thought of Anna and there she was, I turned to the priests and said, "Your god has kept your high priest, "she said, "that Jonathan is now her head priest and that she listens." This caused a stir for a few moments.

Then one of the priests said, "your majesty it looks as if the gods have sided with this god, we are powerless against the gods my lord." He yelled at them, to get out, and then started yelling for more guards to come and kill us all.

I was getting mad so I yelled back at the prince; "you your majesty have no honor, and if you do not stop what you are doing and start showing others some honor I will take you to a place where no one will give you honor ether."

He laughed as he said, "I will watch them kill you with no honor and throw your body to the dogs I believe you to be no god, or you would have shown me the honor that is my birth right even the gods bow before me." The room was filling up with guards I knew I could not fight them all. So I did the next best thing I jumped to right behind the prince with a knife to his throat. I said, "Anna, tell this poppas oaf I will spell his blood before the first one of you dies. And I just talk to his god so there will be no moving on for him."

Anna yelled back, "I don't know what those words are?"

I said, "Just tell him what I said without the words you don't know." I stuck the point in just enough to draw blood, he yelled and everyone froze.

I yelled, "Anna, come here." It took a few moments before I could tell she was moving and every time she would get stopped I poked the knife a little deeper. When she got here she told me what I already knew the prince was cursing me to my grave and telling me how my family Friends and anyone that ever knew me was going to die!

I smiled at Anna as I said, "would you like to get away from here," she giggled as she said, "yes." "Me too," I replied.

Chapter 8

I grabbed hold of her and the prince and we disappeared. When I heard the noise I knew we were there, I don't know why when I jump I always close my eyes. When I opened them I could have leaped for joy, I was home. We appeared in the middle of the side walk in Times Square. Anyone who hasn't been here can't fully realize the ebb and flow of the people here. Walking the side walk with hundreds of people, never touching unless you want to or you're a tourist. Leave it to New Yorkers to have three people just appear and no one notices, maybe a curse or two for getting in the way. But just like any obstacle the flow just parts and go around without people looking up from their phone call, tablets, and papers. The prince laid flat on the cement crying and lamenting his poor turn of luck.

I said, "To him I hope you like it here for this is where you go if you have no honor." I didn't get to go on because I heard the call of angels (well one angel) I heard the call of a hot dog vendor. It took me but just a minute to find him and his cart,

I grabbed Anna by the hand and said, "Come with me I got to have one of those."

She said, "what about the prince?"

I looked down at the man lying on the cement and said, "He isn't going anywhere." I pulled her along till I was standing in front of the device of deliverance.

The man said, "what will it be buddy?"

I reach back to check yes my wallet was still there. I almost yelled out "two sauerkraut dogs please all the way."

He went straight to work like a true artist. When he was done he handed them to me and said, "how about her."

I looked at Anna who was watching everything with wide eye wonder.

Then she asked, "Me; what is that. I explained this is a food of the land and he is an artist in the making. "

The guy butted in saying, "hay what gives man."

I tapped my ear and said "new tech implants but only works for us. She has never seen these before she just got here from overseas, and this will be her first taste of America, so let's give her one plain."

He said, "Are you mad buddy I don't serve plain to first timers, I too, came to this country and look at what it has given me." He talked on and I translated some of it to her, but while he talked he made her a hot dog with lots of different stuff on it when he was done he stuck his hand out in her direction with the for mentioned dog cradle in wrapping paper. She looked at it then at me I shook my head and said "he made it for you so take it, it is a gift." She reached with both hands took it like a holy object, then nibbled on one end, her face lit up like a kid at Christmas, she took a bit this time, smiled and babbled about how great that was.

I started to tell the vendor when he held up a hand saying mister, "I don't need you to tell me what that look means." I pulled my wallet out to pay when he turned to the next guy in line and said, "That show was worth a couple of dogs show your girl a good time while she is here."

As I was shoved out of the way I said, "Hey buddy I will be back thanks."

She started right after she finished her dog with the questions. "Is this your world? Do you live near here? Can we eat other foods? Are they all as good as this?"

I answered all questions by saying "I think we need to save the prince first don't you?" I had pointed to the prince who had caught hold of someone leg that had walked to close and the guy was cursing like a sailor and kicking with his other foot trying to get free. I walked up and said "hay buddy quit kicking him and I can get him to let go."

The guy stopped looked at me and said "is this thing yours you need to keep him on a leash."

I said "hay prince look here."

Anna repeated it a couple of time before the prince looked up when he seen me he looked at who had been kicking him then crawled over to me and latched on to my leg the guy walked off saying "you two need to get a room" then flipped me the bird has he left.

I held out my arm and said, "It is time we go."

Anna gave me a pouty face and said, "Do we have to so quick."

I said, "Yes we are not here to sight see."
She walked up to me and I laid my arm over her
grabbing her shoulder and we ported again. When
I opened my eyes I was looking at the god of
knowledge shrine, with some maidens running for
cover. I laughed and told Anna to till them to
leave us alone while we are here. She left. The
prince looked around then relaxed and set back he
started to move when I took my sword from it
scabbard and stuck it in the ground by his legs. He
got the idea and quit moving.

Anna came back and said "it is done my
lord; girls are set on the stairs and house to be sure
we stay alone."

I thanked her then I turned to the prince and
said, "this is my temple grounds and town if
anything happens to it I will take out my wrath on
whoever the army belong to, do you understand."
He nodded yes I said, "Good! Now prince you are
a man with no honor and I am here to help you or
condemn you the choice will be yours."

He set straight as he said, "I do have honor,
and it is you who doesn't have any honor."

I set back and breathed hard to relax myself,
this is not going to be easy, so let's try a different

tack. I said, "I know you were born with a heavy load to bear, you as prince are responsible for a whole nation, every man women and child is dependent on you, your honor is tied to a million people, everyone says they honor you but you know they just want something from you. And yet you have people who will dress you, feed you, and do your every whim and why not you are the future leader, king, and god. But with all of that what honor do you really have, because they all want something, you are using them like a blanket at night, and they know that as well. So tell me great prince what honor do you have?" I had him on that one and he knew it so he said nothing. So I asked him a question, "what did the captain say that was worth his life?"

The prince moved back and forth for a minute or two then he grinned, he came before me and said "he had a demon caller and if I valued my life I would forsake this land to the demon that lived there." I got up slowly till I was standing, I was looking at Anna when I said "I give up I won't be lied to so I will take him to a world of no honor or truth, I need you to stay here for I am not sure I could get you out if you went."

She repeated every word before saying as "my lords ask I will do."

I reached for the collar of the prince, he moved back. He had wide eyes, and sweat running down his face. I reached again this time I caught it, I turned like I was closing my eyes when he started crying like a little baby and with every sob he was saying "I am sorry, I am sorry, I lied."

I let go and said, "I know you lied and if you do it again I will banish you to a place worst then I took you last time." I set down next to Anna looking at the prince thinking, what am I doing? And why isn't it working? Then it hit me, I stood up and bowed to the shrine and said out load "thanks man you really came through with this one." I turned to the prince so I was looking down at him when I said, "I know the problem you have no honor. I think you don't even know what honor is."

He set back with a defiant look on his face and said, "I do to have honor I have lots of people who honor me."

I laughed there that proves my point, you have less honor then this women here pointing to

Anna. I turned and bowed to Anna, "I am sorry I don't mean that negatively against you." I turned back to the prince before going on. "So I am going to show you what honor is," I said to Anna would you please call one of the girls we scared when we popped in here? She yelled at the house calling someone by name and waving her arm to come here. The youngest girl came out on the porch, so I waved my arm and she came running with a frown on her face.

I know she was trying to think about what she had done wrong now. When she got here she stood next to the prince then bowed before saying, "did you call me my lord?"

I said. "Yes, I did thank you for coming." I got down on my knees then bowed to the girl as I said "I am sorry I scared you and your friends I didn't mean to, but I did so I am asking for you to forgive me." I had my head down but I would have loved to watch how that played across all their faces.

Then I heard the girl say, in a soft voice please "master we were scared till we seen it was you, we didn't know that we had made you feel bad we would never want that."

I set back on my feet to find I was looking the girl in the face with concern in her eyes.

I said, "So you forgive this old man?"

She said with tears forming in her eyes "yes master of course we all forgive you." Then she leaned forward and gave me a hug, I hugged her back.

When she let go I looked around to see a confused prince and a grinning Anna. I said to the girl "I would like to ask a favor if I could, would you mind fixing us some tea please, I have gotten thirsty in my travels today."

Her face changed instantly to joy as she said, "yes my lord it will be my honor," then she got quit again when she ask me, "is this a demon you have caught my lord?"

I shook my head "no this is the crown prince he will be ruler someday."

She got a look of fear then stepped away all most behind me before making a quick bow and announcing" I will bring the tea when ready" and ran to the house.

When she made the house I turned to the prince and said, "That is honor. First I did something that took my honor, so by asking her forgiveness I made it possible to repair what I have done. She then gave me honor when she accepted my apology. Then when I ask for her to fix us some tea she gave me some honor by excepting to serve us. When she returns, I will honor her by thanking her, for her service."

The prince said, "I do not know what you mean I have servants that do what I say every day and I don't have to thank them it is their honor to serve me."

I said, "It is their honor; you are giving it away with no return so you are the loser, or a man without honor."

He said, "I do have honor no man has more than me.

I said, "Ok why then can you not understand me but this woman can? I said to Anna "quit translating for a moment will you." She bowed her head but said nothing. I said, "Ok Prince now tell me what I am saying? He set there looking at me then at Anna then back at me.

He said something; I looked to Anna who said "he says why can't you understand him."

I smiled, "because, you are not worthy of talking direct to a god. You know what If I was your god and I was to protect you I would have quit a long time ago. I bet you have never even thanked your goddess for her protection, what kind of honor is that?"

He said, "I have to; I have priests to honor our god."

I laughed, "So you have given the honor to other to talk to her and she hates to be referred to as a guy. So if I get this right you don't honor her and you depend on others to tell you what it is she wants from you, yes I would have quit protecting you a long time ago."

The Prince began to look scared I didn't catch on till Anna said "I think he believes he might be in danger."

I said, "Tell him he is safe for I have told his goddess that I would protect him while he is in my care unless I banish him." The tea arrive she gave me a cup and gave Anna a cup but set the cup in front of the prince, I bowed and said, "I thank you for the tea."

She bowed and said, "it is my honor my lord." Then she ran back to the house.

"See this is what I am saying when you were a demon she stood right next to you but when she found out you were the crown prince she is more scared of you then a demon, what does that tell you." I picked up my tea and took a sip saying "man she makes good tea," I told Anna. She nodded as she sipped hers. I looked at the prince who was just staring at the cup like it was a demon. I said, "what wrong prince try it you will like it."

The prince said, "I cannot without a tester it may be poisoned."

I said, "Ok I will taste it for you."

He said, "no you are a god poison may not affect you."

I said, "Would the maiden that runs this place be ok? "

He nodded. I heard Anna yell before I ask her to. The head mistress started our way so I told the prince; "I will ask her to but you will bow to her to show honor in the doing or you can do without the tea."

When she got there I ask her if she would mind testing the tea for the prince, she gave him a hard look with his head down before saying "yes." She took the cup off the ground put it to her lips and took a sip the prince looked up when she did it.

I ask "is that ok?"

He said "yes, that will do she can give me a drink now."

The head mistress looked trapped, so she looked at me I shook my head no. She didn't know what to do, you could see it in her face so I reached out and took the cup, bowed before saying "thank you for your service my lady," she bowed back ask if I needed anything else.

I said "no" she look at the prince then hurried to the house. I set the cup back down on the ground, than told the prince there is your tea it is safe to drink then picked up my own cup and took a drink.

He said, "Where is the servant to feed me?"

I said, "No servant here you can feed yourself."

He pointed to Anna and said in an authoritative voice, "you give me a drink."

I stood and shouted "NO" so loud that it echoed off the mountain side. When I looked down both the prince and Anna was face down with hands out I guessed I scared both I will have to fix that later, but I said to the prince "that is not one of your servants that is my voice, a very lovely voice but still my voice, my voice cannot and will not serve you." He had started inching backwards I think I was still yelling. I looked at Anna who was looking at me holding her ground she also had a pink tint to her face, so she got the lovely part, but had quit translating. I calmed myself, turned to the prince and set down. I sipped the cup of tea till I could feel my heart beat slowdown. When I spoke to the prince I had my voice back under control. I went on like nothing had happened, saying "when you have someone else feed you, you give honor you don't have and you make them in charge at that moment. So to seem important you turn into their puppet, you do as they say to get a drink turn as they want you to get feed, you dress the way they dress you, you can complain but still you have what they want to give you nothing more. So prince I don't want a puppet today so pick up the saucer like this (I showed him mine) then take the handle like I am doing put it to your lips carful it is warm and drink." He got all excited when he finally took a drink, you could tell this was a new thing for the prince, we set their relatively quit while we drank our tea, before we finished the little temple maiden came running out of the house with a plate of cookies. She stopped and bowed as she said, "I have made you some cookies my lord."

They were not round, as a matter of fact they weren't even uniformed but I smiled and bowed then told her that it was just what we needed. I took one and tried it. They may not have looked that good but what they lacked in looks they made up for it in taste. I took the plate and a couple more before offering some to Anna, she took a few then I offered it to the prince who with some hesitation took one.

I said. "Do you need it tasted for you?"

He shook his head no pointing to Anna, he said "she already did that."

I didn't point out that was a different cookie because I think he already knew that. This time he surprised me when he bowed to the maiden and said, "thank you." We all almost dropped dead.

The temple maiden bowed back saying" it was my pleaser your majesty." She turned and ran back to the house, with the plate of cookies.

I looked at the prince who had a smile on his face, one I knew well but I think was new to the prince. I said, "Prince that is honor at work, you honored her for real and she is honoring you right now."

His smile went away as he asked, "I don't understand how she is honoring me?"

I smiled and said, "ok let's look at this you honored her because she made you a cookie and you meant it when you did it right?" He nodded ok, "now she has left taking our cookies with her but she is right now telling everyone in the house that you honored her by thanking her for the cookies, she is honoring you to others right now; also she will grow up remembering this moment telling her husband, children, grand children, ECT. So you will be honored for her life time. That honor is now yours to build on or to throw away with the next demand. Remember that only happens if you are honoring someone for a real deed, a fake honoring is well a fake. We set there quit for a few moments before the prince spoke.

"My lord can I ask a question?"

I said, "I am here to teach my lord what is your question?"

He fumbled with his hands for what seemed like forever before busting out "I have been thinking about what you said, about my god and what she does for me, plus you taking my high priest to her because he was doing wrong, so was he doing me wrong too? I think that like eating I may need to take charge of my own prayers so could you tell me how to talk to a god?"

Anna got it out before breaking into laughter, the prince looked offended then confused before realizing his mistake then started bowing asking for forgiveness and crying at the same time. I started laughing myself I couldn't help myself it was funny.

When I could get myself under control I said, "Your prayers are yours there is no right or wrong way to pray, the important thing is in truth because if you lie to a god they quit listening to you. The nice thing about talking to your god you can tell them everything from things you don't like to your own ambitions. They will or won't help that is up to them but you still have a friend."

The prince set up when he said, "Can I do it here?" I looked at the shrine we were setting in front of and started running that through my head. I finally decided I needed more info and I knew the perfect guy to talk too. I stood up told Anna for them to talk I would be right back pictured where I wanted to go and disappeared. When I opened my eyes I wasn't were I thought I was going to be I was looking at the god of knowledge setting in a recliner, with popcorn, a drink of some kind on a little table next to him, watching what looked like tv.

He smiled but didn't get up when he said, "I knew I would see you again but not so soon, but that's ok pull up a chair the game is just coming on."

I said, "I would love to really but I am in the middle of something I need to ask a simple question then I am gone."

He rolled his eyes as he set up, then looking up at me said ok what is it?

I said, "Can anyone pray at a shine to any god?"

He stopped moving a moment then in a serious voice said, "It can be done but not normally it would depend on who you want to talk to."

I smiled as I said "the prince would like to pray to his goddess."

He fell out of the chair with that one. He got to his hands and knees before answering, "I don't mind if he uses mine but I don't know about her."

Then I heard her voice right behind my ear. "I don't like it, and I can't believe that he ask to do it." I shrugged as she walk around me to set in the chair that had been offered to me I bowed, "I didn't know what to do I didn't want to make him wait so what do I need to do to make this work?" She thought a moment before answering but she didn't speak to me but the god on the floor.

"Will you see if the other gods would mind me setting up a small shrine on your hill?" He nodded then disappeared. She went on like she didn't even notice he was gone. "I will have to have a priest there of course; this could be a vacation spot for me. You built your shrine so I think I will try it."

I broke in, "I would like to ask, for a favor I know I am not worthy of such."

She laughed as she said, "you are the most worthy, I now am in your dept three times I will repay you don't you think I won't."

I went on before I lost my nerve. "If you put a priest there he will take charge of the temple grounds for he will be male and I don't think that would be fair." She was looking at me when I shut up.

She had a sweet smiled turned her head to the side just a little and with a mocking voice said, "Are you worried about the poor little girls?"

I was scared but stood my ground when I said, "yes!"

She lost her innocent girl looked and then said, "You are right of course but I have the perfect priest in mind."

With that the god of knowledge popped back and said, "Who is right?" When he didn't get an answer, he said, "no objection your highness."

"Good," she said with a big smile, "now if I could get the god of honor to deliver a message for me I think we could get started."

I started to say "I don't know the language" but stopped myself when I realized I was standing in front of a big room of priest or monks I don't know the different. One monk had his back to me and I think talking or praying to or with all the others, he was looking over his shoulder at me just a moment before falling to the ground and sliding backwards towards the other monks. I just stood there till he made himself part of the group, well stood there isn't quite right for I was standing about four or five feet in the air above, The Alter looking down on the room. When I started speaking it wasn't me it was her with my voice I understood everything but said nothing She said, "Jonathan I am your goddess" she said her name to them but I heard Elizabeth, "I have chosen you to bring back my honor that was taken from me by your former unworthy leader I will not allow that to happen again, serve me faithfully and I will reward you, dishonor me and I will consume your very souls." That last part made me shiver. I could feel all of the priests or monks thoughts as she was speaking and if I thought on a certain feeling I could see that man face and could hear his thoughts. Most were worried about something they had done and if she was going to curse them and praying that they would turn over a new leaf from now on if she would forgive them.

Then she changed subjects and her voice was happy again, "where is *****" this time the name was Japanese with no translation.

A young priest from the back said, "I am here," he didn't move but my eyes went straight to him. She asked him to come forward to kneel with Jonathan. This took a while for it is hard to get through the crowd and harder if you are trying to crawl when you do it.

When he made it to the front she said, "I am giving you a great honor, I have built myself a shrine in ***" she said the name of the village, "I want you to go and take care of my shrine and my worshippers. You will be in charge of my shrine and will help out with the rest of the duties of the temple under the guidance of" I heard head mistress but knew she said her name and by the reaction some kind of title not given to women. There was some murmuring but I looked out to the group and it quickly subsided.

When I looked back down the priest said, "He was unworthy but would be honored to do her bidding."

She turned to Jonathan again this time to say, "You will be sure he has what he needs to get started and go to check on him every so often."

He said, "Yes" and we were back in the clouds. She was smiling setting in the recliner looking at me saying "I had never thought about building my own shrine but you did it and it looked like fun so I did to. So now I owe you again I will have to think on a special gift to pay you back."

I bowed and said, "It was nothing your highness you don't have to go to any trouble on my account it was my honor to do it."

I bowed again she waved a hand and said "till another time then and you need to go, you are interrupting the game." She said, a name and the god of knowledge appeared in his chair she looked over and said "turn this up I want to hear the game," that is all I heard as a door appeared and I stepped through right between Anna and the prince. Who didn't see a thing they were looking over to one corner where when I left was an overgrown field now set a very large shrine, with flowers and fountains!

Anna finally seen me she pointed "did you do that" she asked?

I shook my head no then said pointing to the prince "his goddess did that so he could pray, that is quit a lady."

The prince looked up at me with wide eyes and said, "Is that for me?"

I nodded as I said, "yes and you owe thanks to all the gods in the temple for they opened up their temple to your goddess, she on turn built you a temple so you could say your prayers, what I am saying to you is that all the gods not just one or two listen and care for all they watch, and watch over everyone that includes you so what have you been showing the gods my friend? I have come a long way to meet you, I have come to help you, but I will go then it is up to you what man or emperor you become." I reached down and took the prince's hand, then we walked over to the shrine, we bowed to gather then I said "go talk with your goddess tell her I said very nice." I bowed again then backed up till I got to the temple maidens who were knelt at the edge of what was the field; I touched the arm of the head mistress and said "do you have a minute?" We went back to the house where I told her everything about the shrine and the priest who was coming. The prince walked back from the shrine and I could see on his face he was different from before, just has he got to me I was about to say something when I heard it, the guy I left on the wall holding my first aid kit said in my head "lord if you are coming back please do so soon or I will be joining you."

I could feel the fear in his voice so I said, "looks like it is time to go home prince." Anna took hold of my arm like we where go for a walk I liked the feel of that, then I held my hand out for the prince who took it this time and stayed standing I was just beginning to picture where I wanted to go when I heard a voice yelling to wait I don't mean Anna translated it to me I heard wait plain as day from the girl who had served us cookies earlier. I stopped and looked to see her running to us when she got there she had to breath a moment before she said as always sorry, I don't know why all conversation start with sorry here. Anna had to translate everything after the wait but I think it fell into the god code somewhere. (I need a copy of that thing if I can find it.) She gave each of us a cloth sack with cookies in it and said "this is for your travels."

We all bowed then I pictured where we started this adventure from and was off.

Chapter 9

How we didn't land on someone is a miracle, the room was full of guards with swords drawn even though there wasn't room to swing them, the ripple effect of three more showing up didn't help, then who we where was just another problem so the guards turned their weapons on us. I could just make out the poor guy trying to protect my kit and not kill his own men plus being wounded and I think he was about to lose the fight, so I shoved Anna into the prince and said "protect her" and jumped in front of the guard on the ground and took over the fight. I pushed the two fighting back which was hard considering there was no place to go then the air in the room changed the fighting stopped that meant the two that was battling me quit swinging (it was the only battle.) I reached back to the guard who gave me back my kit, I turned so I could keep an eye on the other two and bowed, while saying thank you but I knew he didn't understand me then jumped back to the prince and Anna. A circle had opened up around the prince with a corridor leading to the door the prince and Anna were holding on to each other I had to smile I wish I could take a picture of this. I heard a voice in my head say consider it done buddy. (That was the God of Knowledge's voice.) Then a big man came into the room must have been six, six if a foot around him was an army of monks he walked up to the prince looking around taking stock of the situation before speaking this man was sharp and I could tell he wasn't used to making rash judgments or statements. But it was a surprise to him and me when all the monks hit the ground with hands out at me, this brought his gaze to me then at them and back I heard Anna voice on the ground as she told me that was the princes father The Emperor, I reach down and picked Anna up then put her behind me. I heard the head monk talking to The Emperor that is when I realized I knew him too that was Jonathan. The emperor walked over to stand in front of me I bowed or leaned forward he did the same to the same amount, yes I have played this game before with royalty, if you don't bow you are being disrespectful to much bow and you are weak, so always a game of inches. I stepped aside so he could see Anna holding my hand flat I said, "This is my voice, and ears in this

107

realm my lord," then I stepped back in front of Anna. He nodded his head at her before I covered her up again. He started the introductions by saying he was the emperor of this land the son of so and so of the family of such and such he had a list of such and suches I listened and Anna translated when it came to my turn I kept it simple I just said, "I am the god of honor and truth." I said it like that should be enough explaining of who I was.

He looked back behind him to the monks on the ground, when he turned back he said, "I am honored you would visit such a humble home as mine but why did you come?" I pointed to the prince, "he was a man with no honor he knew not what honor truly was so I have came to save, if possible this man and maybe your kingdom." I didn't bow, I didn't blink, this was going to be where we find out if I was right about him or was I going to die trying to protect the people that are with me.

His voice didn't change when he addressed me, "so my dear god what have you decided?"

" You my lord have honor you know the difference between false honor and real honor you know that you must give honor to those you meet or you will not have honor yourself this is as it should be, this man on the floor over there is also a man of honor and would give his life to protect."

The emperor looked around seeing all the solders he waved his hand and they all lined up against the wall when he seen the guard he said, "that is as it should be for he is the master of the imperil guards." He bowed a head his direction.

I said, "The Captain over there and the prince here are learning what honor is; now I hope that they remember the lessons given for many will be watching them."

He raised an eye brow before asking "many?"

I said, "Yes for many Gods now know your son and will be watching to see him grow and with him goes the kingdom my lord."

He looked at his son as I finished my statement. Turned back to me bowed a little deeper and said "as it should be I will leave you now if anything you desire while you are here just ask and it will be yours."

This time I bowed lower then he had when I said, "I thank the lord of this land, for your kindness.

He turned and floated through the sea of monks then out the door. The sea of monks started to flow out the door behind him, when I ask "Jonathan is the young priest still here or is he gone already."

The monk turned around "I am sorry for his late departure but he is still here my lord."

I said, "That is fine could I see him here before I go?"

The monk said, "of course my lord he is on his way." Then he finished by crawling backwards out the door. When the room cleared or I should say when the monks left because all the guards stayed at the wall at attention.

Anna said, "my lord have you been here before?"

I said, "Yes I meet them while delivering a message from their goddess."

She said, "Without me?"

Somehow I felt guilty like I had done something wrong but all I could say was "she did the transporting and the talking not me." I turned looking for a way out of this conversation when I seen the master of arms still lying on his side. Walked over bent down and helped the man to his feet, I couldn't let go or he would fall so I did the next best thing I looked at the two book-ends already standing there, I said in my best military voice (yes I don't know how it sounded from Anna) "what a disgrace leaving your captain laying on the ground, step over here and hold him up!" Both men stiffened then side stepped till they were under the captain and I could let go. I checked the bandages they held and the bleeding had stopped I said "ok, this is good do you live in the barracks or a house?"

His replied, "I am married and live in a house."

I nodded and said, "Good I think captain it is time for you to call it a day, you will need to go home and rest let the wife take care of you, no lifting or work of any kind. When the sun goes down you will change those bandages with clean white cloth that your wife has boiled in hot water and dried, the old bandages you will burn." I picked up the second stripped I had cut earlier rolled it up then put it in his pocket. "You are off for the week captain you will not go back to work till that time is over, then light duty. You will tell someone what to do, don't do it. In thirty days you should be fine and getting slow and fat so it will be time to start working out. If you have any problems take three stones stack them, then do it again a hands width apart, and then put a line between them then give me a call, if I can I will send help."(That last part I didn't even think about or mean saying I think I got some divine help I hope it works) I looked at both men holding him up then said to them "you heard the instructions so here are some for you I want you to take him home without hurting him too much. When you get him home you will follow his wife's direction on where and how to put him, you will tell her what I just told the captain is that clear."

Both men said "yes."

I added, "And if you do not do as I have said I will be very unhappy and an unhappy god is not good for you!" I smiled at the captain saying "goodbye friend may you have a long and fruitful life." I bowed so did he with help then the trio was off. I walked back to the prince when we heard the running, it was the young priest he hit the floor at full speed he slide into the room apologizing for being late. The Prince and I both laughed. I told the young man to stand and walk over to the prince and I, don't tell me you can't we just seen you run down the hall." The young man stood but bowed walked over to us and got back down facing me. I looked to the prince and said "this is the young man who will be taking care of the shrine the goddess built for you." I know I just gave more status to the prince but it was still true.

The young man rotated on the floor to face the prince with a little more excitement in his body posture the prince slide forward till he could have touched the young man then he said "Look up so I might see your face." The young man looked up but when he seen he was looking eye to eye with the prince I think he almost passed out. Then the real shook took place the prince bowed and said, "I am honored to meet someone that was pick by the goddess herself, I know that you will take care of all the people in your care and if you need anything please send a message to me and I will see you have it."

I turned so my back was at the young man but was facing the prince then said quietly "Prince I know of a young captain that already knows the people of the village and he already as the ok from the god of that village to enter, that also would with the solders under his control would be a nice force to protect the village from those that would deface it. The young priest then would also be able to arrive safely and timely. Just an idea that's all."

He nodded then called the young Captain over then told him "You are to take charge of the young priest safety then the safety of the village," plus a lot more, when he was done both priest and captain were smiling.

I remember what the captains dream was and this would almost for sure put an end to that so when it was over I walk so I could address the captain alone, then ask "are you all right I know this was not your dream."

He looked at me then bowed to the floor but his voice was that of a kid at Christmas," I have been given something a lot better than that, I can't believe my good luck, I shall sing your praises for the rest of my life. My lord you have given me something I didn't even know friends, and a village what more could a man want."

I bowed then went back to the prince I bowed to the prince when I said, "you have the means to become a great man but now it is up to you, take charge of your own life, live with honor and be true full in all you do this is all I can do so I must go and I will remember you and pray to your goddess for a long and healthy life."

When I stood up the prince was looking sad and he ask, if I could stay and dine with him.

I declined "I have been gone long enough, my time in this era is coming to a close so I must finish all my business before then," I stood took Anna by the arm said "Captain have a safe journey." Closed my eyes and left the world of the prince.

Chapter   10

We appeared in front of the shrine for the God of Knowledge, I guess this is my anchor point if I think of the temple in general. I told Anna I am tired and just wanted a bath, then go to bed, she told me she would be sure my bath was prepared then ran off to the house. I bowed to the shrine and said, "I am thankful for your help and who won the game?" I heard his voice but he didn't say who won, just she is a shark don't ever bet with her, she took it all that women is a monster.

I smiled and said, "So you had fun did you."

The voice came back, "yes she will be here next week to watch finals you are welcome if you want to come."

I smiled, "we will see but I think I might be home by then if I am you and her can come there and I will supply the beer."

The voice said, "Beer what a waste I will bring the liquor you bring the treats.

I said "ok."

I turned to go when the voice said "I thank you for your friendship and honest work to help these people."

I turned bowed again then said, "I was honored, and learned a lot my friend, my dream is that I can keep the friendships that have grown on this trip." I turned and hurried to a bath and a warm bed.

The next few days we went back to the same routine couple of hours in the box to hear the concerns of the village but I started to turn that over to the village elder I was spending more time with nothing to do I would go set at the rivers goddess shrine I would talk about everything I could hear the river bubble in my ears it was calming. I was spending enough time there that I stacked some rocks with a log between for a bench to set on. Anna become busy doing other stuff that she wouldn't tell me, I had spent enough time with her that I realized I was in love with her and the only reason I hadn't gone home was her, but it wouldn't be fair to ask her to come with me and I can't stay here this is what I talked to the river goddess about mostly.

One day Anna came out to set with me she said, "I don't know anything about you.

I said, "Ok like what?"

"Do you have parents? Is the girl you promised too one you like? What's it like to be a god? What is it…?

I stopped her, "ok, ok, let's start slow here. Yes I have parents only one is a live, they are farmers, I have brothers and sisters, I live in New York the place I took you and the prince too, we are not promised in my world we choose our own mates, no I don't have a girl friend never got around to looking or found the right one. Let's see what else oh ya! I have been a god for the time I have been here so mostly I feel out of my depths as a god, when I go home I will be just another guy in a big city again."

She smiled great big has she got up said, "that is good then she rephrased it by saying that is enough for now I would like to know more, but I got things to do." She ran off, I don't mean walked fast she ran like the wind was chasing her. I heard the river laugh. The next day I had the elder in the box as I told him my time was short, I told him all about me and the favor I was asking not just him but his family to do for me, I told him about the medallion and that when I gave it to him I would not be bond to this time nor would I return in his life time, I was honored to have the chance to know him and would feel safe leaving the village in his care. We both bowed and I left the box for the last time. That night was a sad night at the temple because small towns don't keep secrets. I had two of the girls offer to go with me, I hugged all; including the head mistress who was crying (so was I) the only one not crying much was Anna. I was somewhat disappointed but I guess this is going to be a relief not following me around talking and repeating everything that is said I don't think things will go back to the way they were but still this is a peaceful honest life that my family would enjoy but I would be unhappy here if I didn't know it was temporary at least that is what I told myself. When I am setting on my bench I caught myself thinking I could live here with Anna, that's it I leave tomorrow. The captain showed up in the morning with the priest in tow I was able to get that they had talked a lot about gods and religion I was glad to see both I hugged them and gave them a bad time that they came just to see me off, at the boxes the whole village showed up, there was a small ceremony then I stood to take the floor but no Anna I wandered what had happened to her, maybe this is the best for me anyway, I came alone without knowing the language I shall leave the same way. I took the ribbon that held the medallion off my neck then gently place it on the elders neck, turned to the crowd bowed my deepest bow straightened up closed my eyes thought of my apartment then the noise of New York was in my ears. The only thing was this time it was different, for the first time I ran into something when I landed, the bump was hard enough to jar my teeth. I opened my eyes to see what I hit to see Anna face looking back. I looked around the room yes I was home so was Anna I panicked I grabbed and Anna shouted "what have you done I can't take you home you are two hundred or so years in your future."

She smiled at me and in a soft voice said, "Are you still a god here?"

I shook my head "no."

"You told me this is a place you can choose your mate I have chosen you. You are now my home and future. I am your voice and your voice goes were you do. Don't you want me?"

I said in a pleading voice because I was losing my will power "yes I want you I didn't want to take your family away from you." She started looking around the room because she knew she had won at that point, but said "you cannot take family away from me but is it not right that any bride loses her family to make a new one, my family will always be with me but you are mine to take care of and protect every young girl see that a man needs a strong women to help him or he will get lost."

"I gave up," called the office and Jane to find out what was up and to let her know I was home with a new girlfriend, she ran right over to meet this girl and I got to play translator for the evening.

Chapter 11

Three years went by before we knew it. It took one and a half of those years for paperwork, the Japanese government sent a carrier to deliver a package of paperwork that cleared up all the red tape, somehow she became part of the royal family I think that the prince had a hand in that, the wedding was grand and big, heads of states that I never meet had to come. My mom even though I don't think she believed my story took her in so much that most of the time I was the in-law and she was their daughter. I was known as being one of the top authorities on the ancient God of honor and truth, you would not believe how much I have to argue who the god of honor was or was about, I have learned a lot about myself from other scholars.

We decided to return to the village before the baby came, oh ya! She is six months along doctors didn't like the ideal of traveling but she was insistent so here we are in a cab driving into the city from the airport. We were almost to what was the main road into the village. We have been driving on the road that was the only road into town when we were here just three years ago (for us). Why are all cab drivers tour guides? The cab came to a stop at a light because the road stopped you had to turn left or right.

The cab driver said, "That in front of you is the first village, the whole village was said to be protected by the god of honor. The only ones aloud to live in the village are dissidents of the people who live there back then."

Anna said, "So there are people that still live there?"

He said without looking "yes madam there is. The only changes were electric and water. The whole town is considered a temple but the old temple on the hill also got gas. I think the gas line had to run through the edge of the Temple grounds."

Anna said, "We want to get off here." I looked at her she had that look that I know all too well.

The driver was looking at me I said "what the lady wants she gets."

The driver pulled over. I thanked the gods we packed light, I tipped the driver and we walked up to the village gate. At the gate I began to notice in the cement were lines, By following these lines I finally realized what I was looking at, when I knew what It was then looking at it was clear, one side of the walk way there was three stones, the other side had three stones all set in cement, between the two piles of stone was a line, with boxes on one side lined with flowers.

I walked over to the boxes but before I could step into one of them a young priest came up to me and asks, "Do you knew anything about the god of honor." I think he was used to no because he went on, "this is the shrine built by his own hands, it is where he would come and stand in the box there (pointing to the one I almost stepped into) then villagers would come and stand in the other square to be judged where he would reward or condemn the person." I heard Anna in the back ground make a noise.

He turned to look then look back so I asked; "what is the smaller one for?"

He said, "That has been a mystery for years but most scholars' say that it was where he kept the gifts he would give out."

I asked, "What do you think it was for?"

He shook his head before saying "I don't know but for some reason I think their wrong. I would like someday to know for sure and it has always been my dream to meet the god of honor there is a rumor that he will return one day."

I looked at Anna who was almost laughing out loud. I gently pulled at his arm I said, "can you stand in that box right there?" He was reluctant but finally stepped into the box. I stepped into the other box, Anna slipped into the small box. I went into my teach mode as Anna named it. I said, "These boxes are a place of honor and truth only, so you could bring any dispute here and talk only of truth with honor towards the other then when you step out you then can start again with the knowledge of the other parties' truth." As I told him this I switched to English, Anna repeated and translated as before even though I am fluent in Japanese and she in English "the small box was for his voice one of the temple maidens he choose to be such. I think that with your prayers tonight to your god that you may find you have meet him and he is pleased with your service, but need to improve your facts to help all that come here." I stepped out of the box helped Anna step over the flowers picked up our bags then entered the village. Again the god of the village was back.

We walked down the path (for it was a road no more) and talked, I said to Anna, "they don't know you, and we will probably be thrown out on our ears you know that don't you?"

She said, "We will see but I don't think so." When we got to the house she didn't even pause walked right up to the door and knocked, when they opened the door, she ask for the oldest women in the house, that we were family but only she would know. There was some discussion before a women of seventy or so came to the door Anna bowed and said "I am she who is the voice of a God, the daughter that has walked in time, come home."

The old woman eyes got as big as saucers she looked Anna up then down as the tears came to her eyes, she said, "Anna?" I thought I was smart but she left a code so that whenever we came home they would know she was family, the old woman looked at me then asked Anna "so this is the god of honor."

I looked around no one could hear so I walked up bowed and said "my name is Bill glad to meet you."

She bowed then said "come in family should not be left outside," she moved and we came in then it was like at mom and dads.

Anna became the middle of attention and I found a seat off to one side with most avoiding me. I notice a girl looking around the corner of a door screen then someone behind her pushed, her into the middle of the opening before she could stop, she then rushed back behind the door there was a small scuffle before her head came back to look around the door again. I got up and slowly walked till I could not be seen from the door, then slowly slide along the wall till I was on this side of the door and she the other, then I jumped out and around the door saying "BOO!" I was surprised because there must have been half a dozen kids behind that wall. They scattered yelling and running all but one, the one that had been looking around the corner she was in a ball on the floor crying. I picked her up in my arms and walked back to my chair, the mother I think, got up and said walking my way," what's the matter?"

I held up a hand she looked at me then at Anna. Anna nodded her head and the lady (not happy,) set back down watching me. I held the child to me saying "I didn't mean to scare you this bad."

She stopped crying and said in a soft voice "you did to."

I laughed "so this is a act is it there will be payment taken for you dishonesty" I started tickling her, on her ribs then she would turn so I got the other ribs we were laughing all over that chair I had my hands full just trying to keep from dropping her.

I stopped before she hit the ground she turned, looking at me in the eyes and said "are you rally a god?" I heard her mother say from across the room "Anna you don't ask things like that."

I smiled at her mother and then at little Anna "it is all right, I am your uncle so you can ask me anything you want," but the room had got silent everyone wanted to know the answer to that question, but Little Anna said "you don't look like a god to me."

I had to ask "so what does a god look like?

She got a serious look on her face as she started waving her arm while saying "they are big and scary, and then they take you away if you are bad."

I said "have you been bad?"

She looked unsure before shaking her head "no."

I laughed as I said, "then you have nothing to worry about do you."

This didn't cheer her up but she did get closer before whispering my Grandma said, "That you took people away and didn't bring them back." I could see her mother move toward me but Anna still smiling put out an arm to grasp her dress to stop her.

I said, "Those people were bad and they lied to me and others, you don't lie do you?" She shook her head "good then you have nothing to fear from me or any other god for gods are here to help you and protect you."

She smile and said" you too?"

I smiled back "of course I am your family and that's what families do.

She thought about that for a while then with a grin asked "so are you a god or not?"

I started tickling her again and said "not right now, I am your uncle from America right now." I tickled her till we both had tears from laughing when we got our breath back, I said "it is my turn to ask you a question who are you named after?"

She pointed at Big Anna and said "her."

I said "did you know that name is special to me."

She shook her head but said "they make fun of my name at school; no one has a name like mine."

I smiled even though she was looking down and frowning I gave her a hug then told her "that was the name I choose to give to her when I came the first time so it is a name that I love above all others, so now you share a name with her pointing at Anna, that makes you special to me too. Do you want to know a secret, you got to promise not to tell?" She nodded her head with big eyes so I said in a whisper "Anna is not her real first name I gave that to her." Her head turned to Anna's than back was about to call me on it but before she could I called out to Anna and said "Anna what is your real first name?" Anna didn't even pause when she said her full name in Japanese, so I looked back at the girl with surprise on her face, then I said "that makes you special because Anna the name I love is your name and will be all your life." I gave her a hug then said "remember it is a secret." She nodded her head and I set her on the floor. I told her to go play; I needed to visit some old friends while I am here. I stood walked over to big Anna gave her a kiss before saying "I am off I don't think I will be long."

She smiled bobbed her head before saying we will be staying here so no hurry, "tell them Hi from me."

I said, "I would," then headed for the door when one of them ask what friends does he have here? I slowed down I wanted to hear Anna's answer. She didn't even bat an eye when she said "the gods on the hill of course" I left.

Chapter 12

The walk up the hill seamed harder than just three years ago (well to me anyway) the crowd was different mostly tourist but a few older people. Those looked at me like I was different than the others but I couldn't be. When I got to the gate the walk way to the house was lined with booths or wood walls or something, the land was still in good shape there was a few temple maidens around I could tell by their dress, there was a couple of priest too, one of those fell into step with me at the archway into the temple grounds. He just started telling me about the history of the temple that the whole town was under the protection of the god of honor, a fierce god who saved this village from destruction from the army of the emperor himself. I stopped him when I seen the house for they had built something across the front of it.

I said, "Doesn't anybody live in the house?"

He said, "yes the twelve gods live there no man may enter and only the temple maidens can go in to clean and set out food for them each day, there is said that one god even has his belonging set up in the big room but alas I am not allowed inside so have never seen it for myself."

I said, "So how do they get in if this is blocked?"

He smiled "there is a back door."

I said, "Ok so how do I go to the other shrines to pay them homage?"

He said, "All gods are represented on the path but if you would like to see around the temple I will let you in."

I told him I did then walked straight to my old friends shrine, I pulled a book from my pocket placing it on the rocks at the base of the shrine then said "I have brought you all pictures of Anna and my wedding to look at, I sure have missed…

 I was interrupted by the priest who said "you can't put that there."

I said, "why not it is for him."

He was flustered but said "all offering need to be made at the main offering table."

I again said "why they will all see it, if they want to that is. He reached for it again and I said, "That is not a good idea I think you will make him mad if you do that. He stopped just inches from the picture album, and then pulled his arm back when it burst into flame's the fire was brief but hot, and then the ashes did a tornado style dance before disappearing.

He was in shock and on the ground when he lifted his head and asked "who are you?"

I smiled and said as I stepped through the door that had appeared "I am the god of honor."

I stepped through the door to look straight in the face of my old friend the god of knowledge. He was looking at me but something was different more godly, handsome, taller watch in my opinion was bad because he started too tall anyway. I said, "What happened to you?"

He said "I have been raised to a greater minor god."

I smiled and said "how did you pull that one off."

He smiled "I didn't but there is someone else that you got to see."

I turned to see this tall slender woman with a tear drop running down her dress and a small crown on her head. When I say running it was moving from top to bottom with scenes of different kinds of fish, snails, rocks. Waterfalls, you get the picture yes it was the goddess of streams and rivers.

I bowed and said, "I missed you, I set up a small place back home but I didn't know if it worked or not. I am happy for both of you and I am glad life is good, But why the change in status then?"

"Why! Because I am the god who gives knowledge to gods, and she gives comfort to the same gods." And yet neither of us has gained as much status as the god we both serve.

I ask (looking around them trying to see if someone else is hiding here) "who is that?"

They both laughed I felt the joke was on me somehow then he said, "you of course, you have the respect of a major god and minor gods, but if you don't believe me look at yourself."

I looked down at myself I just wish I could look this good all the time. I said shaking my head "I don't understand."

The god of knowledge patted me on the shoulder and said "I will enlighten you later right now I want to see those pictures." So the goddess of the rivers and the god of knowledge and I started walking, going I don't know where, when they both just stopped well that not quit right she stopped first looked at him when he looked around he then said "oh I forgot please call me Bob and her Benzaiten those are our names, with that we have turned over power to you for there is power in someone's true name."

I bowed and said "I am deeply honored so please let me share my name with you it is Bill." We all bowed then walked on till I could see a group of people all turned in looking at something. When I got there they opened up so I could see one of the picture in the photo album, the god of the mountain said "you are a dork man."

I smiled it's all I could do because he slapped me on the back so hard I think I lost a year or two of my life. It and I was passed around for a time, then I ended up in a chair with Bob, I said "when I get home you will have to come watch some games at my house you still owe me."

He said, "Great I would like to see your American football."

I said, "good it is the right time of year let say the Sunday after I get home," then I thought of something "is it going to be a problem traveling to America?"

He said "no I already was a traveling God but when you put those shines up I then could travel there so can the god of rivers."

I said "I will look forward to it and you can meet Anna face to face." I heard a voice in my ear" saying "I will be there to and I liked the pictures." I looked around but no one was there it didn't matter I knew the voice so the god of protection of royals was coming too.

I stood then said "I am glad I came but I need to go now."

The god of knowledge said "you know you can port or jump here at anytime right?"

I shook my head no he just laughed. There is one more god you must meet. I said, "I am tired so can I put it off."

He shook his head this time, but said "you miss understand when I said must meet I mean for you to leave you must meet."

"Oh!" I said, "I get it ok where too." He pointed behind me how does everyone come from behind me? She was short but had an air of government regulator about her. The god of knowledge said "do you remember when the jokester said let her cover that up", I shook my head yes, "good let me introduce the god of protector of gods."

I said "really?"

She spoke like a small drill sergeant, "yes I protect you gods, you just do as you please and I am left cleaning up the mess look I have a priest who just meet his god, another priest at this moment is praying madly because he just seen the god of honor walk into a shrine. I have a whole family that knows that you are real and married to the great something grandmother. If I don't keep this in check there will be a riot of people trying to see the god. People will die."

I started to explain but she put up a hand. "I have heard it all before and I know you are new but can you give me a break already, I can do nothing about the priests or temple workers, their job is to care for the gods, and your family is your family plus with that little secret code I think they will keep it quiet, besides when you leave if they say anything most will not believe."

I said "there is something I think needs to be fixed mostly by the ones who teach."

She nodded "I understand that is the way of gods but do not let anyone else that is not a worker for the gods know or I will have to do something drastic."

I looked at the god of knowledge he said "she destroyed a whole village a couple of times."

She nodded "ok do you understand?"

I said "I did" then she just disappeared but her voice stayed for a minute and said "the priest at the gate will start his new teachings but will not remember you till you cross your lines out of the village." Then even the voice was gone.

We walked back to the door when we got there he said "I have one more gift for you but not from me. It is from that woman that protects royalty she said she owes you so she came up with a very good gift to get even."

I said "you two still running around to gather?"

He shrugged she knows her sports and knows how to have fun, many gods don't." He then brought out from behind his back a sword it was the fanciest sword I had ever seen. He said "take care with this sword it was made for the gods and I don't mean us this thing will cut through any man made material and most god-made. It will never get dull, having this sword is a calling card saying you are a major God, some of them may take offence to you wielding it, but no man or god can take this from you even if you die the sword will stay at your side. You my friend are entering the legend group of hero's."

I said "I am not a hero; I help people that is all."

He smiled but with a sad smile "that is the definition of a hero my friend."

Chapter 13

I stepped through the door next to the priest I didn't look down he didn't look up but I said "can I see the house now? No hold on! Second thought stay or come don't really matter much to me I have to thank someone right now." I turned and walked to her shrine knelt then said "I am grateful but you didn't have to go to this much expense for me, I was always honored to be helpful to you." I stood then started looking around at the shrine I made one lap, then two, then three, the flowers were died some of the stones were out of place or missing the more I looked the madder I got till I walked up to the priest on the ground looking up at me I could till he had no idea what I was getting upset about, but still I couldn't see why mine was taken care of and hers wasn't so I said "who is responsible for taking care of this shrine?" If he wasn't on rock I think he would have dug a hole with his bare hands crawled in then covered himself up. I felt like fire was coming from my eyes as I looked down on him he was stuttering a lot before he got out "we all do my lord." This took me back they all did this should be under the royal family priests. I asked in a calmer voice I hoped because I still didn't feel calm, "where is the priest from the royal family?"

Still stuttering he replied "there has been no one from the capital for as long as I have been here my lord."

My temper flare again but not at this guy I turned to the shine and said "I will get to the bottom of this my lady don't you worry about it", I turned my head to the priest this time I said "don't move I will be back" then I was gone. I had pictured the cathedral but no people just the view I had last time of the church, sure enough that worked for there I was in mid air again with three priest on their faces praising their goddess, I didn't introduce myself I said in a load voice "where is the head priest?" The echo told me I had said his name but I didn't know his name so I had help, I looked up and said quietly "thank you." I settled down on the floor and began to walk back and forth across the front of the church, when I noticed what I was doing I knew I had to calm down or this wasn't going to go well. So I said "I don't know if you can hear me Benzaiten but I need to calm down fast and you are the only one I know that can do it here." I felt it start at my head like taking a cool shower; it ran down my whole body taking the stress with it. I could feel the calm returning to my thoughts. I pictured her she was smiling I bowed in my head and told her thank you she walked over to me putting her head up close then she was gone and I was dry except one drop on my check.

At that moment the priest bust in to the hall, one hurried my way looking not pleased, and the others slowly disappeared back behind the door. He got to me didn't bow or introduce himself he just started yelling. "Who do you think you are barging in like this and what kind of theatrics are you pulling you nearly scared my priest to death," he went on I just listened till he was done or in till he seen I was smiling, he then paused before asking "what do you want sir?"

I said in a calm voice "I came to ask; why you have no priest at the shrine of you goddess in the village of honor?"

He said "you know sir that times are hard, we at the temple feel it too, donations are down and we don't have money to have a priest at every shrine."

I just went on like I was a tourist asking general questions, "but that temple she built with her own hands!"

"Sir I don't know how you got in here but that is just a story told from the old days we know don't we that god or goddesses don't build their own temples or shrines." He put his arm around me to lead me out, and a couple of priest had come out from behind the door.

I just said "I really don't think you know your job," with that I put my arms around him pictured a face and we jumped, just before we left I thought I need to quit doing this. When I opened my eyes I looked around I wasn't in the chapel anymore I was in someone's room, I heard a noise below me so I looked down, there was the face I was looking for, we settled to the floor I walked over tugged on his arm till he stood up than gave him a hug which he returned, I said "I missed you how are you doing?"

He said "I am doing fine I think, if you don't mind me asking my lord why are you here? Am I in trouble my lord?"

I laughed "no not you someone else." I pointed at my guest. He turned and bowed the other guy returned the bow but with no feeling. I said "I need to ask a favor of you if you don't mind," I bowed.

He said "for you anything including my life if you so desirer it."

I said "no nothing like that just some guidance for this man he is the head priest of the order of the goddess of protection of royals, but he has lost his way and I don't think he understands the duties expected of him from his goddess, so would you mind talking to him about what is expected and also he doesn't believe that the shrine that is in my village was built by her. He thinks workers did it."

Jonathan said, "of course it would be my honor and my duty to guide him back to the path that needs to be lived."

I said "you have become quit the priest." I bowed and while I am asking "is the prince here?" He smiled "yes my lord let me get someone to take you to him." When a young boy showed up I was surprised but he was willing.

I started to leave when the man I brought ask, "ok, I give who are you and who is he?"

I slowed down I wanted to hear this. Jonathan said "I am" and he gave his full name and title. He paused for a full minute before going on. "And that man is."

But the guy hit the ground before saying "not the prophet Jonathan He who speaks to the gods!"

Jonathan said "thank you for your kind words but you could say the same thing for yourself."

He looked confused before saying "I don't know what you mean."

Jonathan laughed "that man who just brought you here is a god."

He looked my way I just shrugged then was pulled out the door by a very persistent boy. When I got to the prince he dismissed everyone so it was just him and the master of arms. We talked and the master of arms let me look at his wounds.

I ask "how are you feeling?"

He said "that he still wasn't doing anything, but feels he should be."

I said "ok let's try some practice moves to see how you are doing," I turned towards the Prince "with your leave I think we will go to the court yard."

The Prince said "not without me your not." When we got there I said" I need to barrow a sword."

The master of arms said pointing to my side "you already have one."

I said "I am sorry this is a sword of the gods if I pull it, before I could stop it you and the prince would be dead along with most of your men."

The master of arms said "it is a good thing you had the other sword when we fought isn't it?"

We all laughed, one of the guards gave me a sword we fought but just basic moves when we were done I asked "so how does the wound feel?"

"He said "the wounds are fine my arms and back are killing me."

I laughed again well I think you need to start working out some more if it starts to hurt cut back for a day or so. I hugged them both as we said our goodbye's then I was lead back to the priest and Jonathan. When I got back both were sitting on a bench talking about the troubles of doing what needs to be done without the funds. They stopped when I approached so I said "are you ready to go?"

Jonathan stood gave me a hug before telling me "I will miss you again my lord I pray to you and the goddess always."

I shook my head I hear you my friend (which was one of the things I had to get used to I heard prayers they are like email, the just wait till you are on line) he turned to the priest who hadn't moved yet, then spoke his last words before leaving the room he said "this god can tell you but it is no secret truth my friend to yourself comes first then honor to all around you is the only way for anyone to find true happiness." As he left the room he placed a priest outside the door telling him that no one was to come in till we were gone.

I set down saying, "so have you found the path as they say?"

He said "I don't know there is so much to take in to start with I didn't ever think I would meet the prophet or a god in my life time now I have meet both."

I smiled and said "we are people too, just not all the time."

His head was going up and down but his mind was racing somewhere else so he didn't catch the joke. He turned and I could see tears in his eyes when he said "my lord please forgive me I didn't know you were a god, I know I was rude and that I of all people should have known better, so I deserve being taken as his high priest was. (Pointing to the door that Jonathan went thru).

He looked down and didn't say any more so I said, "look you didn't know better and you didn't believe, I think you do both now, the other guy he did and still did what he did there is a difference, you now have a choice, do as your goddess has instructed or turn in the robes and let someone else lead."

He said "maybe I should step down to let others lead, I thought I was a good priest."

I held up my hand to stop him "sorry my man you have just seen a prophet of old and a god you can leave the order or lead the order but you will never be able to follow someone else who has not seen the things you have. The choice is yours but I have just spent my time while I am on vacation because I think you are a man of honor and truth, the goddess does not make mistakes and she chose you, so again the choice is yours, but telling us we made a mistake is a dangerous thing to do my friend." He started rocking back and forth so I said "look go home talk to your goddess and close friends then decide, but before you make anything final pick a young priest for her shrine then go with him to fix it up and I think you will get your answer. He agreed then we stood I closed my eyes and again entered a room full of people. I looked as four guards pulled their guns and pointed them at me and started yelling for me to lie down and let go of the priest.

I am getting tired of this I spoke into the priest ear "I expect you in two days," closed my eyes and then peace came over the world again.

Chapter 14

The priest was still were I left him I walked to his side before saying "you think you could walk me to the house now, I am tired of all this ruckus." He looked around then at me I smiled "you would have had to have been there" he shrugged then stood and walk in front of me like a man going to his death.

We walked to the back of the house and entered through the kitchen door it was a real door which must have been put in after the time I was here last. The kitchen was new or at least looked new had a natural gas stove, refrigerator, I opened the door it was half full of food and water, the priest said "it is checked daily to be sure that all is up to date and available for the gods who live here."

I said "do they eat a lot these gods that live here."
He shook his head no "they have never eaten any of the food that has been left here."

We moved into the dining room, the table set just like it was when I was here; I asked "why all the plates do you come here to eat?"

He got a shocked looked on his face and started saying "no! We would never try to eat at one of the god's plates, these are set so that one of the twelve gods will always have their place ready, and no mortal can ever set here, because it would offend the twelve gods."

I moved on. When I got to the big room there was my sleeping bag in the middle on a sleeping mat with candles around it. I just said "ok story please."

He said "this is where the god of honor" he stopped before rephrasing "you used to sleep when you were here with the other gods."

I breathed in and out hard before looking up to the ceiling and saying "I am sorry goddess of my protection but they got this so wrong and you did say holy people were ok." With that I looked down walked over to my sleeping bag and pulled it back to the closet, when I opened the door there set a neat stack of cloths that I had left and my back pack, I said out load "I forgot I left this stuff here that means my" I dug in the pack till I found, it my pocket knife, I put it in my pocket. Then I seen a T-shirt that was my favorite so I took it before folding my sleeping bag back out where it should be. I told the priest "this is where I slept that room point into the big room is too big for one guy to sleep in; they did try to make me sleep there though." I walked past the priest into the dining room again "I think it is time for a refresher course on the rules so young priest I have a job for you," he bowed to the ground I rolled my eyes "I want you to bring all of the temple maidens in here, and the head priest of this temple, oh bring everyone that works here."

He said "now my lord."
I looked down at him and said "yes now!"
He bolted out the door; I found my set and set down.

They started coming in looking around like something was going to jump out of the shadows to get them, everyone jumped when they seen me, I said, "have a set anywhere is fine." They started setting at the walls I told them "no at the table please," most objected but I won every time.

When the priest came back he was towing an older gentleman saying "you have been ordered here you must come."

I could hear the other man say "by who and why here." They stopped talking when they came through the door. I pointed with my hand to the two empty sets at the other end of the table.

The first priest said "this is all the maidens and the workers have gone home I can send someone to go get them if you want?" I said "this is good for now I think we can accomplish what I want with this group."

The older gentleman said "who are you to come in here?"

I said "this is my house, this is my temple grounds, and this is my village, I am the god of."

He cut me off turned on the other priest and started shouting "you let a lunatic in here I hope you didn't let him touch anything" the priest started to say something when the older guy went on "you did you let him touch stuff didn't you I should have known and you brought us all in here to share in this disgrace."

The young one finally said "I have seen him at work he is the real god."(The old one started again),

I slowly got up then turned to whisper in the maiden ear on my left "would you mind moving to that spot on my right I think someone else is coming and that is her set." She didn't say a word just crawled around me then back to the table I bowed and thanked her then pictured the face of my lovely voice.

I heard a crush and open my eyes to the lovely face of Anna. I turned to the other ladies Bowed and said "I am sorry I didn't mean to startle anyone," then turned back to Anna before saying "I would like to invite you to tea with me and some others."

I heard someone say" does he do that often?"

Anna smiled "you get used to it" then to me she said "as my lord commands I will do." She held up a hand for me to help her out of what looked like a comfy chair, when I got her standing I whispered in her ear "sense when" I said to the ladies "I will bring her back when we are done." we jumped. I help Anna set down in her spot then stood at mine the men had stopped fighting now the room was looking at me, I ask "are we done fighting now or do we need to wait some more?" No one said anything I took that as they were done, I said "this is my voice and ears, this was her house, temple and village before it was mine," I looked from Anna down the table to find all except the older priest had moved back from the table so they could put their foreheads on the floor and their hands out.

I jumped when out of Anna mouth came a voice that a drill sergeant would be proud of she snapped "temple maidens up." All the maidens set straight up, then "to the table." They all obeyed I don't think that they even knew why. She went on "there are rules to this house you as temple maidens are sworn to live by these rules one is you will not bow before a god in this house or on temple grounds."

The maiden that had moved to my right said "my lady we have never heard of these rules you speak of, when did they came about?" Now Anna looked at me I just spread my hands and bowed to her. So she went on, "the God of honor came to this house and talked with" she said her whole name and her title I just called her head maiden.

The older priest burst in "you are wrong no woman as ever been given that title especially back then."

I broke in this time "there was one, and it was given to her by the goddess of the protection of royals, if you would like (which I am sure you won't) I can make it so you can meet her, the goddess that is."

He said "are you threatening my life."

I said "oh no, I am not you wouldn't be the first priest I have introduce to the goddess, one not so good and three went well."

Anna looked at me with a puzzle in her eyes when she asked "you have taken another one?"

I shrugged "not quit it was close he should be here tomorrow you can meet him then."

Then it struck me I said to the old priest "there will be two other priest here starting tomorrow to work on the goddess's shrine so you will need to arrange rooms for their stay." I turned back to Anna made a bow and hand jester again so she went on.

"They agreed to some rules that all temple maidens will follow and later priest, the first and most important to the god was no bowing or lying on the ground. You will recognize him with a head bow but no more and you will not stop your duties just because he is around, if ask you will do whatever is ask, we are temple maidens our job is to take care of the gods who live here and show honor to all of them, we will at one meal a day set with the god or leader to discuss our lives with each other to get to know each and everyone's want and desires. There will be honor given and truth spoken in this house only. Each of us and each god that we share our lives with here are family." She stopped and I thought she was done then she added "if you meet the god someplace other then on holy ground you will pay him the full respect he is entitle to."

I said "you could have left that off you know."

She looked up but didn't smile "these were the rules that you agreed to, and that we swore to honor are they not?"

I said "yes they are."

She looked back at the girls then "we have no choice but to honor these rules," then she smiled "and it makes us all family to a god.

The old priest not so confident any more spoke "my lady who are you? Because you talk like you were there."

I said "Anna why don't you tell them when you were born and a little bit about your life then go on with the names of everyone who set at this table and a little bit about each of them maybe where they lived, and I will fix us some tea."

She made a face I said "what?" She said "you may be a great god but you make lousy tea." The girl on my right again said "I can make us some tea."
I looked at Anna lost another none verbal fight then bowed to the girl and said "would you honor us by making some tea for us to drink?"

The girl jumped to her feet and ran towards the kitchen then stopped running back she said" it is my honor" than ran off, I could see some of the other girls wished they had been faster

Anna started by telling her birth date and that she was born in the house at the foot of the stairs to the village elder, and at the age of eleven I became a temple maiden one of twelve, then trouble entered their village and her father was about to be killed, when a god showed up and saved her father's life and the village. He chose from the temple maidens' one to be his voice to the people and his ears that one was her. He instead of killing all the unworthy he began to teach starting with my father and the captain who was going to take my father's life, they became good friends. He began to teach the temple maidens what their jobs meant not to the people but to the gods he honored everyone that came he taught that honesty and honor was every one's right and duty.

"It is my honor and duty to show honor where ever I can so I can get honor back. But honest honor only for false honor is just throwing away your honor." I was proud that she had listened all of those times. She went on "then the country needed the god's attention so he went to the capital to save the crown prince who he took from this land to teach him the meaning of honor. When he returned his job here was finished he said his goodbyes and left this village and I went with him. When we got to his lands he made me stay with a women that does his bidding for a year till he was able to make it right to marry me. Then he honored me by letting me carry his child," she said that part and rubbed her tummy for effect I think. I looked down the table yap every one of the women was in love with her I think it was almost worship status. She looked over to me then her face changed as she said "when did you get a new sword?"

I said "it was a gift from the goddess for help in the past."

She then asks, "When did you see her?"

I said "earlier remember the priest I was talking about, I will tell you about it later I think it may be for something in the future, I will have to ask when she comes over."

Anna repeated "comes over?"

I said "oh ya! I forgot to tell you that in three weeks her, the god of knowledge, and the goddess of streams and rivers and possible the goddess of protection of god."

She made a face and said "who?"

"Oh the goddess of the protection of gods, I guess I have been a bad boy about talking with too many people."

Anna said "they are coming where?"

In hindsight I think I should have noticed the warning signs but didn't "our house of course to watch the game Sunday."

She cried "how could you! My house is a wreck and you invite people over not just people but gods."

I said "your house is not a wreck it looks fine by me."

She was shaking her head saying I don't
know how you can say that we just left on
vacation things are not put away the dishes are in
the strainer, there is so much to do before gods
can come to our door." I looked down the table to
find I had gone from god to demon in all of the
temple maidens eyes, must be a girl thing for the
priest looked as lost as I felt.

Then Anna voice changed I had to look to
be sure she was not someone different when she
said "as you command my lord I will do." She had
a smile, and was back to her rosy self for some
reason I don't think I won that one, and the looked
on the temple maidens faces told me I was right.

The tea showed up to save the day because I
didn't know how to move on from there. I tasted
the tea bowed my head at the girl who was just
sitting down and said "this is good tea you have
made us thank you."

She bowed her head back then asked Anna if
she had done that right. Anna said "yes that was
just right." Anna went on by naming each girl
where they set, and where they lived in the
village. Then top it off by telling what was the
plans each girl hoped for that included the head

maiden, some of the girls when Anna said the name would say that is my family or we live in that house.

When Anna was done I said "ok now it is your turn to tell me who you are? And what are your plans for the future?" We started next to Anna and went down her side of the table.

When we got to the old priest he didn't want to answer then he said "to be what I am, I am happy here."

That didn't sound right so I said "let's go over the rules again this is a place of truth, we don't lie to ourselves or to the others here for we have honor for all on an equal bases.

He looked trapped but I didn't let him out we just waited.

He finally said "it is not going to happen I am too old for what my dream is and yet I still have it."

I said "No one here said that they will get there dream but we all still strive for them."

He cleared his throat before saying "I like this temple and have done what I thought was the best for it, I have learned from you things that need to change and I swear they will but my dream was to be over the temple at (He said a name I hadn't ever heard before) but I cannot get a transfer and they don't transfer old priest like myself." He stopped tilted his head back down so he could look at us; he started slowly looking up at the ceiling like he was saying a prayer.

I smiled "now that wasn't that bad, and if you don't ever tell your friends then no one can help you."

We went on to the young priest his was short he said "I love this temple every sense I was a little boy so what I want is his job." Pointing at the old priest, he then bowed and said "I am sorry."

The old priest smiled then said "don't be I will not live forever young man."

That was so touching that I felt I could at least ask where the village is I don't think I can do anything really but as they went to the next in line I looked at the ceiling pictured the face of the god of knowledge and ask "do you know where this temple is?"

He laughed "of course I do, don't you know who you are talking to."

I laughed "will someday I may get a stumper in there."

He said "not today my friend, the temple is just around the mountain from you, it is in bad shape, the grounds or unkempt and no one really goes there anymore. But once it was a great temple."

I said "do you know the gods there."

He laughed again "you know a lot of the gods there for most are the same as here."

"I know you are not a runner but can I ask a favor of you, can you check to see if they would mind a new priest, he really does care for the gods and land he takes care of but sometime forgets why he is doing it."

He disappeared I set there with a blank mind and elevator music playing in my head. When he returned he looked like the cat that ate the canary, he said "they would be honored to take any priest that was offered by the great god of honor."

I laughed "ok what did they really say?"

He said "that is what they said, but there is one catch, they want a shrine in your honor on their grounds."

I said "I don't have time to go build a shrine."

He laughed "you still need to learn the ways of the gods you just have someone else build it, you just bless it when it is done."

I said "ok, I am good with that, now what about the priest that is there?"

His smile went away "no one knows but the gods that the priest that is there has cancer and will not live much longer so if he can help the poor guy till his death then I see no problem."

I said "ok, I think this may solve all problems thank you my friend and that better be good drinks you are bringing or I will get you the worst tasting beer I can find."

He said as he faded out, "I won't answer any more questions if you do." Then he was gone I was back, but the room was quit, so I looked down to a lot of bowed head including Anna's.

I said, "Ok! "What's up? Was I talking out loud?"

Anna said in a soft voice; "who was that you were talking to?"

I answered without thinking "that was the god of knowledge you sure won't find a better god then him." Then my brain caught up to the conversation "you heard him?"

She nodded "we all did."

I said "well that make this simpler" we all were looking at the priest at the end of the table "your job awaits you and the gods there are waiting to." I stood and bowed to him and said "I would be honored if you would build the shrine for me."

He bowed to the floor when he said "I will my lord and I will honor you till I die."

I set down there was no more to say on it I think they can solve the change of command between themselves. I will talk to the head priest who is coming tomorrow to get the paper work to catch up with the facts. We then went on, if I though all surprises was over I was wrong of course.

When we got to the girl next to me that had made the tea when asked what she wanted to be when she grow up she said pointing at Anna "I want to be you."

Anna got that mother look on her face and a smooth voice when she said "child you don't know what you are saying."

The girls said "I do you have got to travel in time; you are married to a god who speaks to other gods and one who loves you, we can all see that. I don't see what there is not to want with that."

Anna face got softer if that is possible when she said "I would not change a thing in my life but the things you forgot is I left all my friends and family in time they grow up and died and I was not part of their lives, I came to a world of things I didn't understand and I didn't speak the language. The god I loved made me stay with a stranger to protect my honor, now I am married to a god whose job it is to go where he is called, if something were to happen to him while he is gone I will not know or be able to go to him if he needs me, for I won't know what place he will be in or time. So my husband can die in time and I will not know I am a widow just that I am alone with a child in a time not mine and that he didn't come back." She smiled but sadly as she took my hand "I would not change my life for anything, for this has always been to me my lord and my lover, but you need to think about your wish my dear girl."

I think all the temple maidens were crying to tell the truth I was about to burst out crying myself. When we were done the girls cleaned up and started washing the dishes the two priests were talking to them self so I broke in to say "I will be going you need to remember to talk to each other daily and honor each other and yourself with the truth always."

I took hold of Anna hand but before we could jump she said "my lord would you mind if we walked down the mountain." The trip down was slow and quit. When we reached the bottom I helped her set down on a bench next to the stairs, she said "my lord would you set with me?"

I did and she tucked under my arm I ask her "what is it again with the; my lord?"

No sound came from Anna for quite a while then in a soft voice she said "I am sorry my lord but I think I need to say this, you are a bigger, more powerful god then I ever knew." I started to say something about I was just learning myself but she stopped me by saying "please, my lord this is hard for me. When I decided to go with you I didn't know if you would even let me stay with you, nor if you would ever love me but from the first time you opened your eyes to now I have never had a reason to doubt ether of them. I am just a peasant girl from a village in your past, you are a mighty but gentle god that travels in time, and yet you treat me and always have like I was the goddess and you just my servant. I worry my lord that this is a dream and that someday I will wake up, I worry that you will go away and find another for your heart, and I worry that you will go someday and get yourself hurt or killed and be alone, that is the one that I fear the most I know you will go again, I know that you will meet others as gods do, I want you to know that my biggest wish my lord is for you to never be alone and always come home to me even if another must follow." She hugged me tightly while I tried to wrap my mind around what she was saying, what was I suppose to say back I didn't know. Then she stood and said "I have said my piece and we will never talk about it again."

I said "hold on don't I have a say in this?"

She looked at me then grinned but just said "no!" Turned and started walking back to her relative's house.

Epilogue

I meet the priests at the front gate when they arrived and explained what I wanted to happen with the old priest and the temple he said he would be sure that it got done by my will.

We stayed a couple more days but I never went up the hill again, it did get troublesome when I would meet one of the temple maidens in the street though. The first priest never recognized me but started teaching the tourist about the temple with the right information. I was told later that he did say once or twice that he meet the god of honor after Anna and I left. Little Anna became my shadow and was really heart broken when we left. Her and her mother came and stayed with us when Anna had the baby. I heard the old priest call my name and I was worried something had happened so I popped in to see and startled a crowd of people at the dedication of the shrine to the god of honor. I could see where a lot of work had been done to the buildings and grounds. There were two priest the one I knew and one I didn't, I talked to both telling them I was pleased with the work they had done. I bowed to them and left. I hear them pray from time to time, the old priest has taken to telling me about the progress on the temple, and visitors, they lost a child one day just to find him taking a nap behind my shrine, I got a new name added to the rest protector of children.

The god of knowledge said "that is ok people do that a lot by them self."

I said "that the baby was born didn't I, well she was a beautiful girl we named her Elizabeth Brook, and made the two Goddess, her god mothers." That I think may have been a mistake. I didn't realize that god parents were so hands on, both want to baby set when Anna and I get a date night, which is nice but we came home one evening to find a miniature river running through the house. I mean it started up stairs in one of the bed rooms flowed out and back so as not to miss any one room, the cascading waterfalls down the stairs with a small bear trying to catch a smaller trout, it ran into the study before stopping in a pool with a very happy baby playing in the middle of it. When the god of rivers seen we were home she raised her hand and the water all drain into the pool and disappeared with no water marks much to the relief of Anna. I didn't mention that we had to move into a bigger more exclusive house, the gods sport night as Anna began to call them was getting quit large for our little apartment, now about the goddess of royals she thinks that Elizabeth is her own private princes, and every princes must have certain things. So at the age of eighteen month my daughter is the most stylish dress women on the planet, she has dresses from dress makes that don't make anything for anyone but royalty. She has designer sleepers, pants, shirts, you get the idea. No outfit would be complete without jewelry of course she has tiaras. Crowns, rings, loose gems for play thing big enough that she can't swallow of course; this includes Anna because no god mother's little princes would be seen with a mother who isn't as stylish as herself. Anna once said she was worried that with all this stuff around that the baby may be in danger from robbers or kidnappers.

I laughed then said, "you really thing that someone is going to get that close to the baby that they don't approve of. I already know the god of knowledge has a portfolio on every one that comes in contact with us and heaven help anyone you does anything to Elizabeth, I already feel sorry for any young man that she falls in love with." We both laughed at that.

On her second birthday my whole family showed up and all the gods, plus a few dignitaries. The party was huge. Did you know that maids can be considered temple maidens, who knew right?

I asked the goddess "what will happen when we have another one."

It was her turn to laugh as she said, "most royals have more than one. "

Elizabeth was two years three months when we got a beat up vanilla envelope with no return address just my name.

I was looking at the unopened envelope when Anna came up and asked "what is it?"

I said "I don't know." I ripped open the top and a coin rolled out into my hand, will bigger then a coin but just a little with strange writing on it that I couldn't read. Anna handed me Elizabeth that she was caring around, turned and left without a word.

I was showing the coin to Elizabeth saying" I will have to ask your uncle about this." When Anna came back, she had my backpack and my old sword.

She said "Elizabeth give daddy a hug and kiss he has to go to work now." Elizabeth gave me a hug and kissed me on the check, then held her arms out to her mommy, who put her on the ground then she gave me a big hug and an even bigger kiss, before saying" hurry back my lord," stood back and bowed, Elizabeth seen mommy do it so she tried to bow herself, it is hard to do and still see.

I looked around then said,

"I love you and don't move the furniture."

I recited my oath and started a new adventure.